Building Benjamin: Naomi's Journey

Barbara M. Britton

This is a work of fiction. Names, characters, places, and incidents either are the product of the author's imagination or are used fictitiously, and any resemblance to actual persons living or dead, business establishments, events, or locales, is entirely coincidental.

Building Benjamin: Naomi's Journey

Contact Information: titleadmin@pelicanbookgroup.com

Cover Art by *Nicola Martinez*

Harbourlight Books, a division of Pelican Ventures, LLC
www.pelicanbookgroup.com PO Box 1738 *Aztec, NM * 87410

Publishing History
First Harbourlight Edition, 2017
Electronic Edition ISBN 978-1-61116-977-5
Paperback Edition ISBN 978-1-61116-883-9
Published in the United States of America

Dedication

To Betsy Norman, thank you for encouraging me to finish this book and challenging me to make it better.

Acknowledgements

This book would not have been possible without the help of so many people. My family has been my cheering section throughout my publishing journey. I am blessed to have their love and encouragement.

A big thank you goes to my editor, Megan Lee, who corrected all my mistakes and perfected this story, and to Nicola Martinez for her continuing support of my writing and for her wise leadership at Pelican.

My marvelous critique partner, Betsy Norman, was at it again. She forced me to keep on churning out chapters and cheered me on until the end. The Barnes & Noble Brainstormers keep me focused on my stories and are a highlight of my week. Thank you, Jill Bevers, Liz Czukas, Karen Miller, Betsy Norman, Liz Steiner, Sandee Turriff, and Christine Welman.

My Mo's Crew friends motivate me to be a better, and faster, writer. Thank you, Justen Hisle, Mary Hughes, Leigh Morgan and Edie Ramer.

I have a huge support system within the WisRWA community, SCBWI community, and the ACFW community. I am grateful. My church family in Wisconsin and countrywide has been a huge blessing to me as always.

And this year I not only have to thank my writing community but also the medical community who helped me overcome breast cancer. I am amazed at the skill and caring of the staff at Froedtert and the Medical College of Wisconsin. How do you thank people who save your life? I will try. Thank you, Dr. Alonzo Walker, Dr. Erin Bishop, Dr. Carmen Bergom, Dr. John Burfeind, and the staff and nurses of the Breast Care Center, the Courage Cancer Center, and 7NT. Cancer has many life-affecting aspects, so I am grateful to Morgan Depas for my genetics counseling, Debbie Grant for helping me be able to use my arms again, and my radiation crew for making sure no bad cells got away.

And last, but definitely not least, to the Lord God Almighty, for giving me the gift of creativity and breath each day to write these stories.

Also Available

Providence: Hannah's Journey

Coming Soon

Jerusalem Rising: Adah's Journey

1

In those days Israel had no king; everyone did as they saw fit. ~ Judges 21:25.

Shiloh, in the land of the tribe of Ephraim

Naomi peeked from behind the tent flap. Girls emerged from scattered booths, illuminated by the flames of the bonfire. The beat of a timbrel echoed over the vineyards while tambourines tinked in thanksgiving to God for an abundant crop. Naomi's stomach hollowed at the thought of joining in the revelry at the harvest celebration. She had never danced before at the feast in a manner to seduce a husband.

Her palms dampened. It was almost time. Time to twirl and catch the eye of a landowner. With two of her brothers slain by the Benjamites, her father needed a bride price.

Movement in the moon-shadowed vineyard caught Naomi's attention. Had a goat gotten loose among the vines? She squinted into the darkened rows of naked stalks. No leaves shook. No trellis gave way. No bleating rang out. *The smoke is deceiving me.* She blinked and retreated from the open flap.

Cuzbi, the merchant's daughter, came close as if to share a secret. Naomi's reflection widened in the gold of Cuzbi's headband. "Do not worry," Cuzbi whispered. "Follow me and the men will line up to give our fathers gifts."

Naomi prayed this was not a lie. Cuzbi had danced the previous harvest, and the one before, but Cuzbi's father had not received a single shekel.

Naomi smoothed a crease in Cuzbi's striped robe. "I will dance in thankfulness to God for a bountiful harvest and let my brother and father deal with any suitor. You will be the bride tonight. I hope your father is prepared for an onslaught."

Cuzbi squared her shoulders, growing even taller. She patted her hip. Jeweled rings glimmered on every finger. "Come, Naomi. Stand as if a jar rests on each shoulder. The drape will show your curves."

Naomi's nerves fluttered like a wounded dove. She brushed a hand over her ringlets. A lone braid kept her curls from obscuring her face. Losing her brothers' wages meant more time at the loom and less time adorning her hair. Her dyed sash would have to entice the spectators, for unlike Cuzbi's adorned robe, Naomi's was pale as a wheat kernel.

Before she could check her appearance in her polished bronze mirror, Cuzbi grabbed Naomi's arm and jerked her out of the tent.

"The men will arrive soon from their feasting." Cuzbi's gaze darted about the clearing as she surveyed the ring of virgins who pranced around the fire. Young women in colorful linen swayed to the music. "Ah, there is an opening near the front of the procession." Cuzbi sprinted into the circle.

Naomi raced after her friend and ducked nearer the fire, next to Cuzbi. Dancers bumped Naomi's side, jostling to be seen by their mothers and ultimately the eligible men making their way from the banquet.

Hurry, Father. How much roasted lamb and wine did the men of Ephraim need?

Waving to her mother, Naomi signaled her arrival into the mass of whirling bodies. A bead of sweat trickled from her temple and slithered down her cheek. She swiped it away and raised her hand in praise to God. She lifted the other and pretended to card wool in the wind.

Cuzbi leapt in the air and swung her arms as if they were waves rolling off the Jordan River.

Not ready to leave the hard ground, Naomi kicked up her heels one at a time, careful not to injure any followers. Her stomach balked at any elaborate jumps.

A scream rose above the music. Then another.

Had someone fallen? Been burned by the fire?

From the fields, half-naked men wrapped in loincloths rushed into the circle of dancers. Naomi froze, even though the tempo of the timbrel remained festive. These were not the bathed and robed men of Ephraim coming to celebrate. These were armed warriors. She breathed a prayer of praise that her surviving brother imbibed at the banquet.

A charging intruder whipped a sling her direction. Covering her head, she crouched under the *whoop, whoop, whoop* of his weapon.

"God protect me," she prayed.

Music stopped. Wailing started. Naomi looked up. A raider scooped Cuzbi off her feet. He slung her over his shoulder as if she were a small child.

"*Regah.* Stop!" Naomi screamed.

The strong-armed man vanished into the surrounding vineyard with her friend.

Another assailant plucked a virgin from the scramble of dancers. Naomi reached to grab hold of the girl's outstretched hand, but a bear of a man blocked her rescue. His weapon whirred in flight above his head. Naomi dove to the side and crashed to the ground, careful to avoid the flames.

Crawling like an asp over a flat-topped boulder, she headed for the fields. A raider grasped at her sleeve. His nails scraped her skin. Pain sizzled down her arm as if embers from the fire had embedded in her flesh.

"*Kelev. Kelev katan.*" The high-pitched insult grew closer. Naomi glanced backward. A scowl-faced boy ran toward her attacker.

Her young savior slashed a pointed stick at the assailant, snaring the leather sling. She had seconds to escape. Praise be to God!

She fled into the harvested rows of vines—in the opposite direction from where Cuzbi had been taken.

Racing along the rows of plants she'd played among as a child, Naomi's heart lodged in her throat, strangling each breath.

Curses trailed after her. Curses about her speed. Curses in…Hebrew? Her own tongue?

Banking right, she panted as if these bandits had also stolen the night air. She sprinted toward the broken trellis, needing a shortcut through the barricade of vines. If she made it to the olive grove, hiding would be easy among the trunks and branches. Had her sole remaining brother been lazy? Or had he replaced the worn trellis before his revelry? She prayed he'd forgotten his duties this once.

Her hand hit the cracked wooden rod. Splintering, it gave way. "*Selah,*" she exclaimed under her breath, for this one time, her brother's laziness was praiseworthy.

Ducking under the greenery of the grape plants, she darted toward the station of olive trees. Her sandals *thapped* against her heels. Certainly the raider would hear her flight, but slowing her pace would put her in peril. Oh, where were the men of Shiloh? Her father? Her brother? And why were these warriors invading a religious celebration?

She passed one olive tree. A second. A third. A fourth. With trembling hands, she beat at the shoots from a tree and buried herself amidst the leaves. She listened for her follower. No footfalls. Good. Her chest burned, greedy for air.

Leaves rustled.

She stilled, but couldn't silence her breaths. In and out they rushed, sounding like a saw on cedar. Old-growth trees were not far away. She scrambled down another aisle for better cover. Grabbing an olive branch, she propelled herself behind a trunk. She hit something hard. The bark? Her forehead ached as though a rock had pelted her skull. Flickers of flame dotted her vision.

When she went to massage her temple, someone seized her arm.

Her stomach cramped. "Leav—"

A palm smothered her lips. The taste of salt and soil seeped into her mouth. Her back struck the prickly growths from the tree. Protests lodged in her throat. Darkness surrounded her, but she kicked at where her captor's legs should be. Banishing the dainty kicks of the dance, she thrashed to do damage. Her attacker did not turn aside. He pinned her to the trunk and held fast.

Lewd taunts grew closer. Her pursuer from the vineyard was in the grove.

Oh, God, do not let me be defiled by one man, let alone two.

"Answer me quietly. Are you one of the virgins?" Her captor's command came forth in Hebrew. He lifted his hand from her mouth, leaving barely enough space to answer.

"Let me go." Her breath rushed out as if it too were fleeing these raiders. "I will slip away. I promise not to alert my people."

"Shhh." Her captor pressed his warm palm over her lips.

"Virgin. Step forth."

Instantly, she was pulled to the ground. Her captor pinned her hips to the dirt with his weight. He lifted her robe. Cool air bathed her knees, sending a chill throughout her body.

She fisted his hair. "Spare me." Even with all her strength, she could not remove him from her body. Her heart pounded louder than a ceremonial drum.

He caged her in the dirt and sent his lips crashing into hers.

She squirmed. Her stomach lurched. Her lungs ached. She needed a breath. She needed a savior.

His weight pressed against her belly. Though he did not take her hem above her thigh. And he did not take her virginity.

"*Argh.*" A roar split the night sky. "Eliab, what are you doing?" The bear-man stood over them, huffing from his pursuit.

Her captor finished his kiss. "Lie still." His words rumbled against her ear. The side of her face prickled from his stubble.

"You mean what *have* I done?" Her captor's body continued to cover hers. "I have taken a wife."

He had not! This man, Eliab, had rested upon her, but he had not joined with her. Although if her father or brother caught him atop her, they would beat him until he claimed her as a wife, or offered a hefty sum. She was not about to call Eliab a liar with her pursuer from the fire crouched over them, staring wickedly. Why had Eliab lied? Was he a friend to the tribe of Ephraim? A friend to a tribe of Israel?

"Go on, Gera." Eliab rose, bearing his weight on his forearms. "Find another. We must leave at once. Hurry. Or do you care to look upon another man?" Eliab's question shot out like a well-aimed arrow.

Gera hesitated. He spat at Eliab's feet and retreated toward the bonfire.

Her spine sank into the ground. Thanks be to God. She reached to right her robe.

Eliab gripped her wrist tighter than a gold band. Realization of his intent sent her heartbeat on another gallop. He had not been a brute, yet he held her prisoner, and he did not seem set on releasing her.

"I am in debt to you. And you will be in debt to my father if he finds you touching me." She tugged against his rigid arm. Her cheeks warmed like stones near a fire pit. "Let go."

"I cannot deny a fellow Benjamite a wife and then fail to claim her for myself." With a jerk, he coiled her into his chest.

Naomi stiffened. The thud, thud, thud in her ears grew louder. "You are a murdering Benjamite?"

"One of the few that remain after the slaughter." His words were sharp as a blade.

Naomi picked up her feet in hopes Eliab would be pulled off balance. He remained rooted to the soil.

"Have you come for revenge?" She grunted her

question while struggling to free herself. She squinted into the vineyards. No legion of rescuers ascended the raised beds. Did the men of Shiloh believe this raid a hoax? "There cannot be enough Benjamites left alive to stand against one tribe of Israel, let alone all the tribes."

"I risked a raid for my survival. Benjamin will not be cut off from God. Our women and children have been slain. Our men ambushed in battle. Are we to have no heirs?" The anger simmering in his reply caused a shiver to rattle her bones.

She thrashed like an unruly child. Eliab held firm. "You were kind to spare me from your Gera. Now double that kindness and let me be on my way."

"Gera's kinsmen brought destruction on our tribe. If a name is to suffer extinction, it should be his, not mine." Eliab yanked her off her feet and heaved her over his shoulder. Her temples pulsed as blood rushed to her brain. Fainting would only make his escape easier. She closed her eyes and concentrated on the darkness.

He cinched his hands around her calves and ran. Fast. His shoulder bludgeoned her belly with every jump and jolt. Her stomach spewed up manna and grapes, burning her throat, and muffling her screams.

When his collarbone was about to impale her side, he righted her next to a mule hidden from sight among the brush. She slumped to the ground.

"If you steal me away from my father, God will punish your sin." Vomit welled in her throat. She swallowed hard. "I did not finish the harvest dance."

Eliab crouched in front of her. His eyes were dark as a clouded night sky and held no mercy. "If I do not take you, one of Israel's tribes will cease to exist. God has more to be angry about than a missed seduction."

Tears blurred her vision. She swung a fist at him, but he dodged her attack. She clawed at his tunic. At least she did not have to fear loosening a loincloth like those scantily clad attackers near the bonfire. "How dare you rip me from my home? Benjamites killed two of my brothers. Do not take the daughter of a grieving man."

He pried her fingers from his garment and pulled her close. "And what will your father do if he believes you are no longer a virgin?"

"There was no union." She beat his chest for emphasis. Her knuckles bruised, yet he barely moved.

He pressed his thumbs into her palms and stilled her assault. "No one will bless a union with a Benjamite. No one will give us their daughters. We are left to kidnap Hebrew women. Since I stole you, your father will be held blameless before the elders of the tribes." He stood and yanked her to her feet.

"My father needs a bride price to buy land." Her words rushed forth. She grabbed his arm. "You have lost family and so have I. Have we not both suffered? Leave me here and be on your way."

"Others may not have been rewarded with a mate tonight. Shall I send you into their bed and disappoint my father?" No joy rang from his words. He did not seem giddy like a bridegroom in a marriage tent.

She stepped backward. Could she outrun him in the darkness? She had to. This was her home. Her land. Her tribe.

He caught her wrist and wrapped it with rope. Stray strands scratched her skin.

"Please." She tensed her muscles and pulled against his weight to no avail. Tears wet her cheeks as he bound her other wrist. "My family—"

"Most of my family is buried in a mountain." He unhitched the mule and snapped the reins.

Her body stilled as if encased in clay. Eliab wasn't listening to her hardship.

Distant shouts echoed from the vineyard.

"Father." Her voice squawked like a strangled pigeon.

Eliab stifled her shouts with a rag. "You can ride the mule or I will drag you behind it. Decide. Now." He turned toward the road. "Hoist the nets."

Was he going to trap her kin like wild beasts?

In a blur, he mounted his ride, still holding the rope as if she were a wayward goat.

How could she leave Shiloh? Leave her mother? Leave her father? Her legs trembled as if the ground shook. She did not take a step.

The mule trotted forward.

With no arms for balance, she fell on her side. Her jaw ached from the gag. Coughing, she tugged on the rope and struggled to rise. If he kicked the animal, she would be dragged through rock and dirt.

Eliab dismounted, swept her into his arms, and sat her sideways on the mule. He had caught her and now he caged her with reins at her back and reins at her chest. His body imprisoned her. He leaned into her arm and slapped the mule's rump. "Hah."

She grabbed the animal's mane, weaving her fingers into the coarse hair for balance.

How could the tribe of Benjamin thieve wives from the tribe of Ephraim? Where was their honor? Where was their shame? And where was God? The feast this night was in His honor.

While Eliab was intent on the terrain, she worked a silver band from her finger and let it slip down her leg, down the mule's withers, to the ground. She would leave a trail for the men of Shiloh.

For what was lost could be found.

2

Naomi's back bowed, unable to hold her upright after hours on an undulating animal. After leaving Shiloh, Eliab had abandoned the road for the hills. The crags and cliffs offered cover but challenged their mule's footing.

Eliab dismounted in a small cavern. A few of his thieving tribesmen waited, huddled in talk. Sobs came from a nearby cave. The black-as-a-starless-night opening kept Naomi from seeing what was happening inside. Naomi slid from the mule and headed toward the entrance. Eliab caught her arm. She thrashed against his hold, unwilling to ignore a tribeswoman suffering at the hands of a wicked Benjamite.

"She is not your concern." Eliab tugged her toward a stone backrest.

Digging her heels into the dirt, she resisted his pull like an ornery goat. He yanked. She squatted. He jerked. She fell. His strength won. She slumped to the ground and sat against a flat-sided rock.

Eliab removed the rag from her mouth and unbound her hands. He seemed confident that she wouldn't run into the desert alone without provisions.

He offered her water from a skin. "I do not mean to be harsh."

"And yet you are." Water dribbled from her mouth as she drank. She would have sworn her cheeks had stretched thin like pulled dough. She handed the skin back to him and then rotated her wrist to ease the numbness.

"I do not know your name." He smoothed a hand over the stubble of a beard. "You know mine because of Gera's rebuke, but we were not properly introduced."

"I believe you are to blame for that."

He crouched, waiting for an answer. In the dim light, his hair seemed lighter than her brown locks, which were almost the shade of a raven's feather. His intent gaze never left her face, and his stoic features made it seem as if he could see her soul.

"I am Naomi *bat* Heriah." Her throat grew tight as she recalled her father's name. "And you are Eliab, a Benjamite bandit who stalks dancing virgins."

"Ahh." He chuckled. "You do know of me. We are not strangers."

Strangers? He touched her as a husband. But he did not force his will on her in the grove. Other men may truly have made themselves her mate. The continuing cries from the cave reminded her of her vulnerability.

She wrapped her arms around her waist and rubbed her wrists against her indigo sash. "Where are you taking me?"

Eliab stood. "Near Gibeah."

"Gibeah?" The name rushed forth. Her brothers had been killed trying to seize the wicked city. "Is it not in ruins?"

"We have settled due east."

Would her brother and father find her outside the city? Did her tribesmen even know where the Benjamites had settled, or that they were the ones who had raided the feast?

Another Benjamite called Eliab's name. He motioned for Eliab to join a group of raiders. Her captor uncoiled the rope from his belt.

She tucked her hands behind her back. Her skin itched at the thought of being bound again.

"Go to your band of thieves. Where would I run to?" His absence meant she'd have time to gain her bearings and leave another trace.

As Eliab joined the Benjamites, a woman was helped off a donkey on the far side of the huddle.

Naomi recognized the height of her friend. Praise God, for Cuzbi was alive. *Selah!* She stood and held out her arms. "Cuzbi, my sister."

Benjamites hushed her greeting.

Cuzbi strolled forward and bestowed a brief hug on Naomi before planting herself on the ground near the worn stones. Her long legs sprawled out before her as if this were a gossip-filled chat in a remote tent. "I fit better on a stallion than on an ass."

Naomi squeezed Cuzbi's hand. Eliab had shown restraint this night, but her friend may not have been afforded the same regard. "You are well otherwise?"

Cuzbi tilted her head upon the boulder as if it were made of linen. "My backside is still riding that animal even though Ashbanel stopped so I could rest. They're half-brothers, your husband and mine." Cuzbi indicated the Benjamite that had summoned Eliab. "Ashbanel is the eldest son of Berek."

How could Cuzbi talk as if this was a normal betrothal among brothers? Naomi placed her hands on Cuzbi's cheeks. No fever could be felt. "Does he have you under a spell, sister? We will not be in the company of these Benjamites much longer. We need to leave something behind for the men of Shiloh to discover." Her heart drummed as she scanned her friend's jewelry. Naomi tried to loosen a gold band from Cuzbi's finger. "One of your rings?"

Cuzbi fisted her hand. "I will not leave a mark. What do I gain if my father comes? Ashbanel is an elder of his tribe. He can claim land and livestock. Soon we will have servants. That is more than I could have hoped for from the men of Shiloh."

How could Cuzbi accept one of these thieves as a suitor? Naomi's ears buzzed like a swarm of locusts as she contemplated her friend's betrayal.

"If this man is an elder, then he is to blame for the murder of our tribesmen and for the massacre of his own." Naomi's voice warbled as she thought of her family's loss. "My brothers are dead. Do you not care that this Ashbanel robbed you from your mother and father and sisters? He is too foul to have been given a wife."

Cuzbi curled her knees under her robe. "Hush, sister. My father would have arranged a marriage soon enough. Who is to say my husband would have stayed in Shiloh?" Cuzbi's voice lowered to a raspy whisper. Her eyes glimmered in the meager moonlight. "Ashbanel saw me come from our tent. He said he knew I was the woman God had chosen for him. If that is true, how can I leave him for an uncertain future?"

Naomi's jaw fell open. "You assist your father in the marketplace. You barter with the best. How can you be wary of an offer of marriage?"

"This was my fourth year to dance at the feast. I've waited long enough." Cuzbi wrapped her arms around her waist as if a breeze had chilled her flesh. "I don't want to wait anymore."

Naomi stood and balanced herself against a

boulder. She grasped her sash and lifted it over her head. An indigo swatch would stand out amid the pale landscape. "My father has lost two sons. He cannot afford to lose me."

Pebbles crunched behind her. She turned to see Ashbanel approaching.

"Why are you disrobing?" Ashbanel's inquiry was as harsh as a whip crack.

Cuzbi jumped to her feet.

"Uh…I'm…" Naomi's stall came out like a moan.

Eliab came alongside his half-brother.

"I am lengthening my robe." Naomi's words flowed together, but her reply held steady despite the pulse of panic charging through her limbs. "Shall my ankles be exposed for all to see?"

Eliab straightened to his full height and grew taller than his half-brother. "Naomi is my concern. She can attend to her needs."

"She is supposed to be seeing to our needs. Do not forget that, brother." Ashbanel summoned Cuzbi with a sweep of his arm.

Naomi hopped out of Ashbanel's path. Her gaze met Cuzbi's. Cuzbi turned away, chin high. Naomi struggled to breathe. How could Cuzbi align with the tribe of Benjamin? Against a friend she had known since birth?

"We must ride." Eliab's hand was heavy upon her shoulder.

Would he touch her later? Make her his wife? Make it so she could never to return to her tribe or family?

Mules spidered into the cavernous hillside. Eliab did not seem in as much of a hurry as his tribesmen. Was he confident in his skill to elude the men of

Shiloh?

As she and Eliab passed the small cave, stuttered cries, shrill and desperate, escaped from inside.

Words from the Law flooded her conscience. Moses had taught her people to do what is right and good in the Lord's sight. How had a tribe of Israel become so perverse? And how had this night become so lawless?

"Naomi?" Eliab stared at her as if she were bewitched. He loosened his grip to help her mount. "Get on the mule."

She was not like Cuzbi. She could not accept the deception and thievery of the Benjamites. And she could not leave a dancer from Shiloh crying in a cave. She ripped free from Eliab and darted into the dark mouth of the mountain.

I cannot forget who I am.

3

Naomi rushed into the cave with her hands outstretched. She tried not to trip or fall or injure herself. Thank God for the moonlight's creep. She scanned the shadows, blinking, listening. Where was the weeping coming from?

Figures huddled beyond the light near a jut in the stone. A form bent over another person, who rocked upon the ground. She guessed the larger figure to be a Benjamite. What was the captor doing to the troubled soul?

Naomi's skin flushed hot as if she lay baking in the noonday sun. She fisted her hands and lunged at the attacker. "Leave her be."

A young man, not much larger than she, backed away, arms raised.

"I have done nothing wrong. She will not keep quiet." His voice cracked at the end of his defense.

"Nothing wrong?" Naomi's shriek reverberated in the cavern. "You snatched her from the festival. That is something." She came face to face with the Benjamite. The boy's breath breezed her cheeks.

"I need her silent. I have tried everything to comfort her. And still—"

"Isa?" Eliab spoke as if he knew the offender.

The boy shuffled toward Eliab. His excuses trailed after him.

"Na-oh-mi," cried the girl huddled on the ground.

She recognized that voice. Naomi knelt and cradled her friend. "Jael, I am here."

"He ripped my tunic." Jael clutched her chest as if wounded in battle.

"How did this happen, Benjamite?" Naomi's question held a hint of accusation. Her temples throbbed as she brushed a hand over Jael's damp hair.

"I tried to help her up," Isa explained. "On the mule. The cloth came apart in my hand. She's been wailing ever since."

Naomi cupped Jael's chin. "Is this the truth?"

Jael nodded.

With no father, brothers, or kinsmen, Jael and her mother were cared for by the generous people of their tribe. And since so many men had died warring with the Benjamites, coins were clutched tightly. Jael's garment was probably threadbare at best.

Eliab strode toward her and Jael. "Repair the tunic swiftly? We must be on our way."

Naomi rose and encouraged Jael to do the same. "I will need the light of the moon and the stars. Restoring the weave will take some time."

"Make haste." Eliab escorted them into the clearing. "You have the blink of a star."

She led Jael to the rock where she and Cuzbi had rested. Jael's garment had separated almost to her waist. Bared breasts would not do with all these vile men around. Naomi folded the linen on each side of the tear and tied the loose threads. Eliab and Isa stood by their mounts, muttering sharp words.

"I was not dancing at the feast," Jael said, her chest rising and falling, testing Naomi's hold. "I had one more year." Jael wiped her cheek. Teardrops wetted Naomi's fingers.

"I know." Naomi pressed Jael's hands on the seams. "Hold here, near to your chest. I am accustomed to proper light when I weave. A belt will help keep this closed." Naomi removed her indigo sash. She bit the edge until it gave way enough to rip into pieces. "I have enough linen to bind your waist. Furthermore, you and I shall have matching head coverings." Two women in colorful dress might hasten a rescue.

"How many knots does it take?" Eliab paced in front of the boy.

"I will finish soon." Soon enough for her brother to scout out her trail.

Naomi wrapped Jael's tiny waist, securing the restored stitching.

"*Shalom,* Naomi." Jael's voice hitched as though she would cry again.

Naomi draped a piece of cloth over Jael's hair. "You are fine, sister. Better dressed than before. When I get back to my loom, yours will be the first robe I make." She kissed Jael's forehead and took her back to where the mules—and the men—were stationed.

Isa traipsed forward. "I was not cruel."

Naomi nodded and bit the inside of her cheek. She did not know this Benjamite, and she did not trust his words, but she did not need another enemy.

Jael embraced her. "You have given me hope."

"Remain strong," Naomi whispered.

Isa took hold of the reins and lifted Jael with ease onto the back of the mule. "*Toda raba,*" he said from atop his mount.

"My friend's thank you is enough." Naomi's stare did not leave the boy's face.

Isa nodded and rode off. The clattering of hooves

on ridge and rock reminded Naomi of the chaos of this night. This evening was supposed to be a time to feast, a time to worship, a time to dance, not a time to invade.

Eliab uncoiled the rope. "Isa tended my father's flocks with my brother, Joshua. His word is trustworthy."

"Must you bind my hands?" Her wrists ached at the thought of the prickly cords.

"You fled from me into the cave. Do I have your word that you will not run from me again?"

Should she vow submission to Eliab? What if she had the opportunity to escape? Were they near the border? Near the lands of the tribe of Benjamin? Or still in the land of Ephraim?

Eliab grabbed her hand and tugged her close.

"Wait." Should she agree? Her confidence began to crumble. "What did I do wrong? Would you not have gone off to help Isa if you thought he were in trouble?"

"Yes, I would have gone." He snapped the rope and removed the gag from his satchel.

Saliva pooled in her mouth. She would not be bound like an untamed animal. Not again.

"I will not run away." She spat out the words as if spitting sand from her mouth. "Do not bind me." She punched Eliab's chest. He did not move. Not one step.

He caught her arm, encircled her waist, and lifted her onto the mule.

"Rest, Naomi. You are a tower of stones. The mule listens to one master." Eliab's arms closed around her, holding her next to his body. His tunic wasn't the most comfortable bed, but his body was warm, and up until this point, he had not harmed her.

She prayed her father would find her before Eliab desired a union and made her his wife.

Fighting sleep's snare proved useless. As the mule swayed side to side, her eyelids became millstones. When her eyes fluttered open, a pomegranate-red ribbon of sky rose above the hills. For a moment, before her body fully awakened, she floated, blissful, believing she was sleeping in her mother's arms, rocking gently, back and forth.

Her head snapped upright. She was not in Shiloh. She was on a mule maneuvering a downward path to a wicked land.

"Ah, you're with me." Eliab sat as straight as a rested merchant carting goods to the market.

"And you're still here."

"I am not a dream."

"You're a curse."

"Good. I chose a quick-witted wife."

"Hah. I have suffered enough for one night." She arched her back to help the mule's descent. The stretch of her muscles gave her new life and new hope of a rescue.

"I haven't heard any complaints in the last hours." His tone was teasing.

Ignoring his remark, she held fast to the mane as the mule reached level ground and trotted around the base of the hill, avoiding an earlier landslide of rocks.

She glanced at the camel-colored cliffs, willing Ephraim's army to be perched there.

Eliab jerked on the reins.

Her cheekbone slammed into his shoulder. She rubbed her face, scowling, until she saw why Eliab had halted. Her heart picked up speed as if she had run down the trail.

Several men surrounded Isa and Jael, taunting and jeering in a foreign tongue.

These were not her people. This was not a search party. These men were bandits.

Eliab raised his right arm. "Leave our brother and sister in peace." His warning hummed in her ear long after his command ceased.

Three strangers advanced toward Eliab, but their stares strayed toward her breast.

Her skin prickled as if their lust had stroked her flesh.

Eliab's rebuke came again in a different dialect. He shortened the reins, leaving excess for a whip. "You and Jael are my sisters," he whispered. "If you say otherwise, Isa and I are dead men and you will be a Moabite's whore."

Her throat cinched. Was not Eliab's company preferable to being forced upon by a gang of pagans?

She turned her head slightly. "As you say, my brother."

4

As the foreigners advanced, Naomi shifted closer to Eliab. The solid tower of his body gave her comfort, but not enough to keep her hands from trembling. Moisture pooled above her lip. Being bound to a Benjamite was shameful enough, but she would never join with a heathen. Never. Not while she had breath.

A Moabite with a toothless grin reached out and touched her robe, rubbing the cloth between his fingers. He bent and sniffed the linen.

She tugged her hem from his grasp.

The other two Moabites chuckled.

Whaaak.

Eliab whipped the scoundrel's hand. The sharp slap panicked the mule and it charged into the larger group of men. "Do not touch my sister. She is intended for another." Eliab spoke in Hebrew followed by a Canaanite dialect.

Another Moabite clawed at her leg.

Naomi jerked backward so as not to be pulled from her mount. She kicked any offender who came close. Eliab continued to lash out with the reins.

"Wait." A gray-haired Moabite shuffled toward their mule.

The toothless man and his fellow criminals halted their attack. The older Moabite, dressed in a dust-covered white robe, waddled closer, looking like an overstuffed sack of flour.

"My cousin erred in his ways. He did not mean to insult your sister." The Moabite's gaze crept over her body. "If…" He fisted a hunk of the mule's mane and nearly grazed Naomi's hand. "She is your sister?"

"Are you branding me a liar?" Eliab spoke as if he chewed leather.

She needed to ease the tension between these two puffed roosters, or her future, and Jael's, would be in peril. At least Eliab and Isa served the same God and observed the same customs. She had calmed the tempers of her brothers many times. What had Cuzbi told her about bartering in the marketplace? Flattery gets you a thicker coin.

She cackled like a fortune teller. Was she mad? Almost. How many times could a woman be stolen in one night? This day, she would need all her skills of persuasion, for she would not let herself be carried off by lusting looters.

"You foolish man." She infused her rebuke with an innocent's charm and a concubine's seduction. "What women do you know that dress as similar as my sister and me?" She indicated a wide-eyed Jael with a sweep of her hand. "My mother dyed these veils herself. Surely it is not so different in your country?" Cocking her head, she pursed her lips and waited for the elder to answer.

The gray-haired leader stepped closer. His dirty garment brushed her knee. "You almost have me convinced." His attentive grin made her skin pimple. He was no idiot, for he knew Hebrew.

"Have you forgotten which side of the Jordan you are on?" Eliab addressed the half-dozen men crowded in the clearing. "This is the land of Ephraim."

"Which you are leaving." The toothless cousin

shifted closer.

So they had not reached the land of Benjamin. Her own tribe ruled these rocks.

"We are on our way to Jericho." Eliab's arm pressed against her waist. His pulse pounded through her garment. In this moment, she would do whatever he asked because she needed his protection to remain pure. "My sister is betrothed to a Benjamite."

"Are there any still living?" The elder Moabite cackled and waved in the direction of his thieves. "And what of my men? None of them will do?"

Not a one.

"Our God forbids it," Isa said.

The Moabites looked as if they had forgotten about the boy.

"You do not worship the God of Abraham, Isaac, and Jacob." Eliab addressed the bandits as if he and Isa had them outnumbered. "May our God strike me down if I give one sister of mine to a worshipper of Chemosh."

"We do not need to wait for your god. We can strike you down." The leader unsheathed a blade from his belt.

Naomi licked her lips. A plea for mercy stuck in her windpipe. *Oh, Lord, spare us from these pagans. Do not send me into the land of a foreign god. Or into the bed of a foreign man.*

"Our father will seek vengeance if his sons are slain and his daughters defiled. Do you desire a war with the tribes of Ephraim, Benjamin, and Reuben? They shall ride out in force." Her voice grew hoarse as she tried to prevent a riot.

"Why should the tribes trouble themselves all because I want to lie with a beautiful woman?" The leader crooked his neck toward Jael. "Or two?"

Naomi clasped a hand over her mouth. Her brothers had never been foul-mouthed around her. How could this man speak filth in front of two women?

She shifted closer to Eliab. Her head bumped his chin.

Eliab eased backward. Was he going to spring from the mule? How could two Benjamites claim victory over this lot of scoundrels? She swept her hand in front of Eliab.

"Is that how your father raised you?" She *tsked* at the leader. "I am offended by your insult. I would have thought better of such a man." Crossing her arms, she turned her face from the elderly bandit and shot a sideward glance toward Eliab. "Allow us to be on our way."

Eliab gave her a brief nod.

"Or challenge my brother."

"Choose your weapon." Eliab leapt from the mule. He stood two heads taller than the sackcloth-draped Moabite. Eliab's hand lingered on a satchel tied to his belt. Little did the pagans know there was a twisted rag in the bag and not a blade.

The leader stepped backward and his belly jiggled. "Why should I upset your sister? Come and sup with us. Then—" The leader took a visual inventory of his men. "You can go."

Naomi had the feeling that "you" did not include her or Jael.

Veins ridged on Eliab's arm. "We must leave—"

"And pray." She slipped from the mule. "It is time for us to worship our God. But we will break bread together. Afterwards." She smiled at the foul-mouthed leader as if he had given her a gold bracelet.

"By all means. Come with me." The leader held out his hand.

"My family must face north toward Bethel. The house of our God."

Eliab clutched her arm and motioned for Isa and Jael to join him. Naomi's fingers tingled from his grip.

"In our tradition, where we pray is holy ground. It must not be defiled by idol worshippers." She batted her lashes at the elder to soften her words, but the leader did not seem interested in her truth. He did, however, seem interested in her.

Jael held Naomi's hand. Naomi gave a slight bow to their foes. "We won't be long."

Eliab selected a spot a fair distance from the Moabites. He faced the cliffs from which they had come. He knelt and indicated for Isa to be on his right and for Naomi to be on his left. Jael crouched next to Naomi.

Now she knew which way led to Bethel and to her home.

"Family, sing the Shema." Eliab looked past her to Jael.

"I am a slinger, not a singer." Isa's growl rumbled from his throat.

Jael's singing unfolded like a blossom, slow to start, but vigorous at the end. "Hear, O Israel. The Lord is our God. The Lord alone."

Isa joined in the prayer.

"I will fight for you, Naomi." Eliab's claim kept rhythm with Isa's notes. "You are my only hope for a future. But we are outnumbered. Without the element of surprise, we cannot win."

"*Selah.*" She sang as if she were still praising God

at the feast and not as a woman petitioning for her life.

"You must capture their attention." Eliab's gaze stayed upon her. He sang, "With all your heart."

"With all my soul. *Selah.*" Her melody died down. "You did not see me at the feast. I am not a temptress."

"You captivated their leader doing nothing but sitting on a mule. Now do it again. And use that snake charmer's voice." His baritone chorused the Shema again. "With all your might."

She raised her hands toward heaven and then bowed with her face to the ground. "You want me to play a harlot."

Eliab called out, "*Shalom.*" He cradled her face in his hands as he bent near her. "You can leave here with me or a Moabite. It's your choice."

"And what of Jael? Or the young man, Isa?" Could she abandon fellow Jews to be killed at the hands of their idol-kissing neighbors?

"Trust me, Naomi." His gaze tore through her like a bronze-tipped arrow. "If you dance, there is a chance we all may survive."

How could she refuse and leave Jael to a life of slavery? Or worse, to a life as a prostitute? Isa and Eliab would be tortured until they died. The blood of Jacob's offspring would be on her conscience. Would God punish her for her cowardice? She had witnessed women waiting by the vineyards for the laborers and their workman's wages. She had seen their vile mannerisms.

She would play the harlot to avoid being one.

"I will dance," she whispered, the words lodging in her throat. "I will be a seductress."

5

Naomi brushed the dust from her robe and faced Eliab. Glancing over his shoulder, she prayed scouts from Ephraim would swoop from the rocky hills and rescue her before she disgraced herself in front of these ruthless foreigners. No such blessing found her. "Where shall I begin my deception?"

"Stroll toward the leader. He cannot keep his gaze from you. Isa and I will sit near the mules." Eliab crouched in front of Jael. "Stay at Naomi's heels. Do not get separated. We cannot come back for you this time."

Jael nodded and nestled closer to Naomi's side.

The sun was not high, but bursts of light blurred Naomi's vision. She closed her eyes. Tempting these scoundrels was her burden alone. No second chances waited.

"Be bold, Naomi. Do not hesitate, or they may become suspicious." Eliab placed a hand on her shoulder. He indicated a spot where she should stand. A spot directly in front of the white-clad elder.

Naomi breathed deep. Even with plenty of fresh air, her heart drummed against her chest. She rubbed her palms together, but with the trembling in her fingers, she could not keep them joined. *Oh, God, forgive me.*

As she sauntered toward the loud-mouthed thieves, she swayed her hips and let her arms dangle with an occasional graze of her thigh. Jael followed a half-step from Naomi's sandals.

Sitting in a semicircle, the Moabites observed their approach with gaping mouths full of meat. They ripped at their food like ravenous dogs, not waiting for prayers to be offered or for their guests to join them at the meal.

She strutted closer to the leader while Eliab and Isa positioned themselves behind the distracted Moabites and nearer to the mules.

"Your prayers are too long." The leader bit into a plum. Purplish bits of fruit sprang from the pagan's mouth while juice dripped into his scraggly beard. "I have missed your company."

Her stomach swirled like a potter's wheel. How could she pretend to care for such a foul-mouthed fool? If he stroked her body, she would vomit. A short distance from the crowd, she stopped to give herself room to escape and to give Eliab room to strike with his sling.

"I am famished." She giggled and touched her breast, imitating the harlots that prowled after her brothers. "And my head covering is loose."

Slipping the indigo cloth from her head, she fanned her hair to the side and drew her fingers slowly through her wavy locks. "Oh," she gasped. "I am undone. Only my mother has seen me as such."

A few men mimicked slurping sounds, yet their mouths were empty of food.

She shuddered. Her lips began to tremble. She pressed them together in a mock smile. Never again would she disgrace herself and her family in this manner. Definitely not later in a Benjamite's bed.

The leader lunged forward and reached for her

hem. "Come and share our mutton and fish."

Naomi dodged his grasp. She flung her head covering to Jael and twirled in a circle as if to entertain. When she sidestepped another touch, her sandal caught her robe. Her shoulder bared briefly. "I am too clumsy." She snorted as if she had drunk too much wine and righted her garment.

Whistling erupted in the clearing.

God, turn Your face from their lust.

"Sit with me, woman." The leader clapped his hands. "We will undress each other."

Naomi's face flushed. What new trick could she use to stall this heathen?

She cast a glance toward Eliab and Isa. They were on their feet. Slings in the air. Her hands shook as she stroked her sleeves. "I can strip down for you."

Please, Eliab. Now!

Eliab and Isa unleashed a barrage of stones into the circle of foreigners. The *whizzz* of rock passing close to Naomi's ear sounded like a hissing pot.

The leader's eyes flared. He slumped toward the ground. Blood spurted from a stone that sank into his skull, and immediately, his white tunic stained scarlet.

"Atta—" Before he could finish his warning, the toothless cousin's head snapped backward. Isa's rock jutted from his temple. The Moabite fell like a plank of cedar.

Threats and curses filled the enclosed clearing.

A high-pitched humming in Naomi's head drowned out the chaos. She moved as if in a vision. Grabbing Jael by the wrist, she charged toward the mules to flee to safety.

Nearing the restless mounts, Naomi fell forward. Her forearms smacked the parched ground. A throbbing ache radiated through her chest. Her leg jerked. She twisted to one side. A heathen, sprawled on the ground, gripped her ankle. His hands slithered under her skirt.

Her body shook as if she had been doused with cold water, but she clenched her hand and aimed a furious punch at his head. "Get off."

He caught her fist.

Jael screamed and kicked the offender in the jaw.

Naomi ripped free as the man shielded his face from Jael's assault.

He sprang to his feet with a vengeance.

Jael attacked. Fast. Her foot landed below his belt. The man crumpled to his knees and cursed the gods.

"Bless you," Naomi said as she took hold of Jael.

Before she knew what was happening, Eliab launched her onto a mount. "You must ride." He lifted Jael snug to her back and slapped the mule's rump. "Go."

Naomi held Eliab in her sight for a moment until the mule lurched around a bend. Eliab had sacrificed his own safety. Her belly fluttered. Would she see him again? What would she do without him in this wilderness? Were there other Moabite bands roaming about that she would have to face alone?

She cast another glance behind Jael. No other donkey followed.

"Keep watch for them, Jael. We will head to higher ground. Toward a hideout." Toward freedom from angry and desperate men.

"Are they dead?" Jael's voice blew away in the breeze.

She fisted the reins. "Someone will find us."

Will they, Lord? And who would they be?

This is not how the plan was supposed to end. She had no knowledge of this territory and no idea how to return to Shiloh. She had slept the latter part of last night in Eliab's lap when he maneuvered the terrain. Retracing the path through the Moabite den was unthinkable. But all would be moot if they did not find water, for this mount had no provisions.

As the mule advanced farther into the lands of the tribe of Benjamin, sweat trickled down Naomi's face. Jael had dropped Naomi's head covering during the fight, and without the linen barrier, the sun scorched her scalp. Yesterday Naomi would have been pleased her indigo cloth left a clue to her whereabouts. Today she needed relief from the heat. She patted the donkey's slick coat and prayed they would find shelter fast.

Jael's head lay heavy upon Naomi's spine.

"We will rest soon and then I will search for a cistern. There has to be water nearby." She hoped her declaration was not a lie.

After a while, Naomi spared the mule the weight of a second rider and walked. Thankfully, the height of the animal blocked some of the sun's rays.

Ahead, an uneven path led into the hills. Naomi guided the mule, keeping the lead tight as the animal's hooves scuffed over unearthed rock. Spying an overhang, she secured the donkey so it could recover in the shade. Jael withdrew and nestled by a boulder.

"Rest and I will go look for water. Grass has sprouted under some of the rocks. There must be a basin nearby."

"If not?" Jael mumbled.

"I will catch a nursing goat and squirt its milk into your mouth."

Jael's cracked lips curved into a half-smile. "You will need me to help you wrestle it."

"Like how you fought the Moabite?" Naomi could still feel the man's fingers mauling her skin. She shook her head as if to remove the memory. "Did you face hardship in the fields?"

Jael nodded. "From some."

"Well, we are not in the vineyards anymore." Naomi raised her arms toward the sky. "We are lost in the lands of Benjamin." She sighed at the unbelievable truth of her words and thumbed a smudge from Jael's cheek.

She borrowed Jael's head covering and went in search of something to drink. A pool had to be nearby. With brush and several paths into the hills, this would be the perfect place for water to collect. At least, she hoped that to be the truth.

Climbing over a landslide of rock, Naomi grasped a jut in the hillside and pulled herself up toward a plateau. Gazing at the rolling hills, her stomach hollowed like she was weightless and the wind could whisk her off her feet and down into the depths. She knelt and crawled closer to the edge, scanning the area she and Jael had crossed. No Eliab. No Isa. No one.

Kneeling in the dirt, she squinted at the sun. "I can't do this alone." Was God listening? She raised her sweat-soaked sleeves. "Show me the way home."

She studied the cliffs for a sign. Anything to point her in the direction she should travel. Heat waves rose from the soil like formations of soldiers streaming into battle. Her eyes burned from the sunlight's glare. All of Israel was the color of sun-bleached bones.

She closed her eyes. The sting of her split lips overwhelmed her senses. Could she even mouth another prayer?

Someone seized her arm. She jerked.

A flash of fright shivered through her body. She screamed, and her hands formed claws, ready for another struggle.

"Naomi."

Eliab towered over her.

She stood and collapsed into him. Her knees threatened to give way. "Oh, Eliab, where have you been?" She didn't want to need Eliab, but in truth, she did need him.

"There are secret routes in the hills. We knew we could catch up to you, so we didn't chance the flatlands. We did not want to be followed." He wrapped an arm around her waist and drew her flush to his body. "So, you are glad to see me?"

She stiffened. She knew she should protest his embrace, but his hold kept her upright.

"Do you have a waterskin?" she mumbled into his tunic.

"Two."

"Then I am glad to see you."

6

Naomi withdrew from Eliab's embrace. Solitude surrounded them on the plateau, and she did not want Eliab to believe her to be as bold as she had portrayed to the Moabites. She tried to excuse her actions, but her mouth was as dry as sunbaked sand. She coughed and clutched at her throat.

Eliab grasped her hand. "Come with me and I will get you a drink. When you are refreshed, we will continue toward Gibeah."

Naomi tore free from Eliab's grasp. She stumbled from the force of her retreat. Her brothers had died bringing judgment upon that city. How could she tromp across their graves? "I will not go to Gibeah."

She darted toward the path she had climbed. At the slope of the incline, gravel gave way beneath her sandals. Careening downward, a scream warbled in her throat. She frantically clawed at the side of the cliff for balance.

"Naomi!" Eliab scaled the terrain and encircled her waist with one arm. He cinched her to his side.

She twisted to break his hold. Field work kept her sure-footed enough to maneuver the rest of the stable terrain. She dashed toward the path. Blood seeped from her lips and into her mouth, bringing the sizzle of salt and the taste of clutched coins.

"I will not dishonor my family by setting foot in that city."

Eliab trekked her direction. "My home is on the outskirts."

"*Your* home is there. Not mine."

"We need only pass by Gibeah. I live to the east." Eliab's voice grew raspy as he propelled her through the clearing. "We will not be long."

Naomi freed herself from Eliab's hold. Her relief at his escape from the Moabites waned. "A breath is too long in that tomb."

Isa strode toward Eliab. "Cease your woman's complaints. We must be on our way soon."

Naomi could not endure much more humiliation. She had been tied like a sheep for a shearing. She had sidled up to heathens like a brazen harlot. She had been driven into the desert without water. Now she was to traipse across cursed ground? She refused to gaze upon the remains of a condemned city.

"Take him on your donkey to Gibeah." She jabbed a finger at Isa. "Jael and I will travel a different path to your home."

Isa shook his head. "You have already slowed us down. We are behind the others. I will not stop." He pitched a pebble off the hill with his left hand.

Naomi chilled at the sight of Isa's precision. "You are a left-handed slinger." The accusation rushed from her lips in one breath.

"Is there any other kind?" Isa grinned as if her observation were a compliment of his prowess.

"My brothers fought alongside the tribe of Judah in the first days of battle."

"Then they died of stupidity, for slingers were stationed in the canyons from which we came." Another stone flew from Isa's hand.

Naomi collapsed on a rock in the shade. Her face

prickled from the heat, but her heart hollowed at Isa's revelation. "What did you make me do?" She cast a glance at Eliab. "I danced where my brothers died?"

"Isa." Eliab lunged forward and slapped a rock from the young man's hand. "Watch your tongue."

Isa brushed the dust from his hands as if he were contemplating some retaliation. None came. He stalked toward Jael and then perched beside her on a ridge of rock. "The truth needs to be told. I will not hide it."

"The truth is you left-handed slingers massacred righteous men. Were you in those cliffs? Did you slay my brothers? Your brothers from Ephraim?" Naomi jumped to her feet. Her throat burned hot as a torch. She squinted up at Eliab. Sunlight blinded her. "I danced like a harlot where my brothers drew their last breaths. I'm as vile as a Benjamite."

Eliab spat on the ground and stomped toward the mules.

"Could my brothers hear my giggles in heaven, Eliab?" Tears filled her eyes. She hated being stolen. She hated being away from her family. She hated being used as a decoy.

Eliab thrust a waterskin at her feet. He did not untie the sinew strap. "Do only Benjamites break the laws of Moses? You are misled if you believe destroying Gibeah was just."

She jerked the skin upward, bumping Eliab's leg.

"All the tribes sent men to fight. Your elders refused to punish murderers. Why don't you ask your brother and father to explain why they did not turn over criminals to the tribal council? Even the prophet spoke against you." She unknotted the tie without his assistance.

"The tribe of Benjamin can take care of its own

grievances. Are the other tribes blameless before God? When you danced at your feast, did the men of Ephraim not lust after virgins?" He crossed his arms.

"I would not know, as your slingers raided the festival before our sinful men arrived."

"You danced well enough to entice Gera. And those heathens."

Naomi took a swig of water and almost choked. Air stayed trapped in her lungs. She coughed and sputtered. Clutching the waterskin, she took a sip to calm her windpipe.

Eliab reached for her, but she withdrew from him.

"If I am so shameful," Naomi rasped, "leave me this provision and be on your way."

He ripped the skin from her hands. "I cannot."

"No, Naomi." The cry came from where Jael hid. "Abide with me."

Isa did his best to hush Jael.

Naomi's stomach cramped as if rope bound it—a rope pulling her toward Gibeah and all its tragedy. She bent at the waist and waited for the pain to pass.

"What about the Levite?" Eliab's words were spoken so softly the breeze could have swept them away with the dust. "He sent his wife into the city square to face a mob of men. Does he not bear any blame? My tribesmen summoned the Levite. Not his woman. Her own husband pushed her into the square. No vengeance was sought against the Levite or his family. Only the tribe of Benjamin."

"My brothers died an honorable death. Your tribal elders refused to hand over the murderers of the Levite's wife. Can a man not travel through the lands of Benjamin without sacrificing his betrothed?" Her throat spasmed as if Eliab had gagged her again.

He gave her back the waterskin. "Too many have suffered for the sins of a few. But know this: I would never send my wife to face a mob who had summoned me. I could not sleep the night while she was abused. It still grieves me that I sent you to distract those Moabites."

She drank slow, content to focus on the animal's hide in her hands and not the man before her. "Do not expect me to pity you or myself. I am full up with enough grief over my brothers."

"And I grieve as well." Eliab held out his hand. It hung there in the air, palm up and open. The wind scattered his dark hair across his face, yet he did not flinch. "I buried my mother, my sisters, and my younger brother. With you, I can start a family and carry on for them. The tribe of Benjamin will begin anew."

She wanted a family, but this was not how her father had planned for her to be given away in marriage. No celebration occurred. No bride price changed hands. If she joined with a Benjamite, her father would disown her.

"I need you, Naomi." Eliab's plea crackled as if he were the one who had choked on the water.

She closed her eyes, unable to look upon Eliab's face. She smothered compassion and stoked the embers of defiance. "I will not be a traitor to my family."

"I would be no better than that coward of a Levite if I leave you here in this wilderness alone and unprotected." Eliab's hand dropped to his side. He opened his satchel and pulled out her indigo head covering, laying it in her lap. "You left this in the struggle. I think you will have need of it."

At least there was no trace of her among the

bodies. Neither was there any trace of her to follow.

She handed him the waterskin and smoothed the cloth against her leg. Fortunately, no blood marred its color.

Gibeah was the last place she wanted to be, but it was the first place the men of Shiloh would scout. She clenched her fists, for if she did not go with Eliab willingly, he would bind her and drag her like a prisoner to the ruins of his city. Her only comfort was that Cuzbi would be with Ashbanel in the household of Berek, east of the city. And Cuzbi's father had gold aplenty to jingle in front of the tribal elders for justice.

"I will travel with you, Eliab, but I will not gaze upon the ruins of Gibeah. My eyes will remain shut." She shouldered past him toward the mules.

Jael hugged Naomi's waist so hard, she almost regurgitated the water she had drunk. Isa beckoned Jael to his mule.

Talk did not babble from Eliab's lips as they traveled south. Perhaps he had said too much already. They had both spoken harsh words and ripped open the tombs of the dead.

Isa forked left on a trail outside of Gibeah.

"Where are they going?" Naomi readied herself to jump from her mule and trail after them.

Eliab steadied her arm. "Isa's dwelling is near my father's house. Your companion will be safe there."

"*Shalom,* sister," she called to her friend. "I will see you soon." Naomi waited for Jael's wide-eyed nod.

She and Eliab carried on a different way, cresting a wide hill.

"The city is up ahead."

Naomi closed her eyes. She gathered the donkey's mane and held tight as their mount ambled downward.

"Why do we have to go near Gibeah when the others have taken a different path?"

Eliab pulled her flat to his chest as the mule struggled against the steepness of the hill. "I want you to understand why we were in your vineyards."

"But you were not in the vineyard." She did not move an inch to the right nor to the left as Eliab's arm rested beneath her breasts. His body warmed her like a brick oven, but she took no pleasure in his closeness. *Distract him.* "You were in the grove. I remember." Her breaths shallowed as they swayed side to side. "Hiding behind a tree."

"And look what I found." His voice rose to the clouds as they hit the flatland at full stride. He could not have sounded more pleased. "You came right to me."

She grabbed his arm for balance and lowered it over her belly button. The weight caused her stomach to jump as if fish spawned inside. She hunched her back so his hold would not be as intimate. "Our meeting was not as it should have been." Her reply was but a wisp. "My father had no say." Closing her eyes, she lost herself in the blackness behind her eyelids and tried to erase the sensation of Eliab's possessive embrace. The ploy almost worked. Almost.

Laughter split the silence. Not Eliab's. Or a man's.

Women were giggling. Naomi hadn't heard such glee since the festival. Were there other women from Shiloh here? If there were, their brothers would seek them out. But surely a girl from Shiloh would not be celebrating her capture with laughter.

Naomi couldn't help herself. She opened her eyes.

Oh, Eliab, you are a liar.

7

The gleeful women carried jars on their shoulders and not on their hips, for their bellies were round and full with Benjamite babies. These women were not from Shiloh. They had been in Gibeah awhile. Their navels protruded like a single grape smothered with cloth. Naomi shuddered to think that soon she could be like them, for Eliab was sure to offer her his bed, and she would do everything in her power to stay out of it. *Spare me, Lord.* She desired a child conceived in love, not anger.

"These women are not from the festival." She glowered at Eliab. "You lied to me. It seems the tribe of Benjamin is already growing. How did this happen?"

"What do I need to explain?" Eliab's brow furrowed.

"Where did these women come from if every woman and every child from your tribe was put to the sword?" Naomi clasped her hands to still their trembling. Was the tribe of Benjamin deceiving everyone? "What is this trickery?"

Eliab let the reins rest on the mule's neck. He braced his hands on his hips.

"These girls are from Jabesh-Gilead. Their tribe did not assemble to pass judgment on us. The council elders gave us their virgins, but there weren't enough for all of us who survived the war. That is why a few elders told us of your festival in Shiloh."

"You stole me from Shiloh at an elder's urging?" Her voice squeaked with outrage. How could the elders have betrayed the daughters of Ephraim? Surely her father was unaware of the raid. No word had passed through the streets of Shiloh, or Cuzbi would have heard the gossip.

"I took a daughter, not a son." He spoke like he selected spices in the marketplace. "If you are of an age to dance, you are of an age to be chosen by a man."

"Not a Benjamite!" Her skin burned hotter than a cooking fire.

Eliab dismounted. "What were we to do when all the tribes vowed not to give their daughters to the lowly Benjamites?" His mocking tone grew harsh. She bristled at his insult to his own people. Back and forth he paced. "No man in Ephraim broke his oath to the elders, or to God. No one gave you to me. That is why our raid was in secret." He strode toward her as if he would plow straight through the mule. His feet halted in front of where she sat, and he held out his hand. "Get down and walk with me."

Was he in his right mind? He talked of her capture as if it did her father a favor and then asked her to accompany him using the voice of a suitor.

"You are mad." She shimmied forward on the mule and farther from his reach.

"I'm mad? If you scoot any higher on that mule, you will ride on its neck." He chuckled, softly at first and then louder as if joining in the revelry of the mothers-to-be.

With each boisterous outburst from Eliab, the hair on her arms rose higher. Did the encounter with the Moabites leave him unbalanced?

The women of Jabesh-Gilead hesitated and looked toward Eliab. They acknowledged him with a tilt of the head and continued on their journey into a wasteland of charred rubble. Children did not play in the streets. No livestock grazed nearby. No teasing, nor braying, nor snorting shattered the eerie calmness. All emotion drained from her body and left her empty like the husk of a katydid.

God, why am I here?

"Did you pay for the women or steal them? And what of the families of these girls?"

Eliab shielded his eyes and regarded the ruins. "Dead." The word echoed over Gibeah's crumbling walls. "They have no family to seek revenge. Or money." His gaze met hers. "Their tribe was punished for not assembling and listening to the charges against Benjamin. With no man alive to give a daughter in marriage, the oath remains intact."

"No wives for Benjamites." She mumbled her understanding. "Unless you steal them."

Eliab splayed his arms wide in front of his birthplace. "Am I to survive a massacre and die without a woman and without an heir? Was all this lawful for the life of one woman?"

Naomi positioned the mule so she did not gape at the ruins of Gibeah. She did not want to picture the aftermath of battle. A battle where women and children bore the brunt of a righteous wrath.

"I am no elder." Her voice strained, but she spoke loud enough for Eliab to hear her answer. "I have to trust the leaders' decision and the decision of my brothers to fight against Benjamin."

"The tribes obeyed the council's command. But every day I am haunted by their wisdom." He paused and indicated a spot in the distance. "I lived west. Beyond that tower of stones. Where the fire pit smokes. Ashbanel and his wife and son lived on the other side of the street." Eliab gave directions as though he were describing a route to a traveler, and not where his family had perished.

What did he expect from her? To survey his homestead? The last resting place of his siblings? She knew the pain of losing loved ones. Pressed down with grief was her heart. She averted her eyes.

Silence fell between them.

"Ahh. Do you smell the figs boiling?" Eliab annoyed her with his loud inhales.

Naomi's stomach gurgled from the citrus-sweet scent. She could not remember the last time she had eaten, but Eliab's banter caused a different churning. A churning of worry. Was this place haunting him?

"My mother made the best paste. My sisters would try to assist her, but they ate more than they prepared." Eliab reminisced as if she knew his kin. "When I came home from the fields, my sisters would run and shout my name. I would pick one up in each arm and lift them into the air. They screeched so loud my mother would chastise me. I believe she thought I would drop one of them. But I never would. And I never did."

Naomi's eyes pooled with tears. If only he realized that she was one of those little girls, but she'd run to her own brothers in a vineyard. "My brothers did the same."

Eliab did not acknowledge her confession. He stationed himself between her and the ruins, talking as if in a trance. "In the morning, my brother Joshua would follow me out to the flocks to relieve Isa.

Everything I did, he imitated. From the carvings on my staff, to the clicks from my mouth. Never did he shadow Ashbanel. Only me." Eliab sniffed and swiped at his cheek. "I will never forget the image of my family burning among the boulders of Gibeah."

Naomi rubbed her arm. A chill swept over her flesh. "I do not know where my brothers are buried. A mass grave holds their bodies and those who fell beside them." Her breaths stuttered. "They live in my memories. Their smiles. Their laughter. Their love."

Eliab stepped closer, but he did not touch her.

Naomi stroked the mule's mane. With every pat, she collected her emotions. She didn't want to give Eliab a reason to comfort her. "I am surprised you did not escape to Rimmon. Is that not where the survivors fled?"

"I left Ashbanel and my father to lead the remnant to Rimmon. Isa went with them. He was never on the cliffs." Eliab gazed upon her as if their argument still lingered in his thoughts.

"I am glad." Her voice steadied as the intimate tales of family faded.

He nodded as if he understood. "I returned to Gibeah with a few select slingers."

"How were you not slain?"

"What fools travel into a slaughter?" Eliab kicked at the ground. "Besides, the rubble was at a smolder. There was nothing left to glean. But remains needed to be buried." He surveyed the darkening sky. "That is what I did before rejoining the others."

"Why are you telling me all of this? Aren't you afraid it will overwhelm your soul?" Tears threatened to dampen her cheeks.

Eliab braced himself against the mule. "I'm scared

if I don't remember, I will forget." He rubbed his eyes. His complexion mottled from the force of his fists. "I want their memory with me forever."

She patted his shoulder, not letting her hand linger, only sharing the pain of loss. "We will remember. In time, I think, God will heal our sorrow. Maybe in time, you will forget the devastation."

He stilled her hand and held it. "I wish I was as certain as you."

At the first stroke of his thumb, she pulled her hand back and rested it in her lap. They shared a heritage, not love.

Eliab took control of the reins and led the mule to the path where Isa and Jael had parted their company.

"It is not far." He cast a glance her direction. "Rest while you can."

Naomi's heartbeat rallied anew. What was to come tonight? Was he not as worn as she? She slipped to the ground, careful that the mule's hooves did not crush her feet. "Why should this animal carry my burden anymore? I am accustomed to the loom and picking grapes. I will join you in a walk." And she would plead weariness later.

Eliab slowed his pace. "I was not in Gibeah when the Levite's wife died. I had taken livestock to Jericho. I know the laws of God and what He expects from His people, and I would have fought against the corruption. I am innocent of the woman's blood."

She wanted to believe Eliab was just. He had protected her in the grove from Gera and again when the Moabites pawed at her clothing. At this moment, she did not see a way to be rid of him, and with the unknown awaiting her in East Gibeah, she needed an ally.

"Was your brother in the city square?" She worried for Cuzbi.

"Half-brother." He coiled the excess rein around his hand. "Ashbanel was not with the crowd of frenzied men."

"I am glad, for I care about my friend and her well-being." Her chin rose as she gave Eliab her best brother-chastising frown.

Eliab regarded her with a lighthearted grin. "I have no doubt you do."

Naomi stood a bit taller. She would take Eliab's comment as praise of her compassion. Had he not spoken of his sisters with a kindhearted tenderness? Perhaps the kindred spirit they shared would allow her to reason with him later.

"What is your brother's name?" Eliab grew serious.

"My brother?" She could not hide the surprise in her voice.

"The one who will come for you. I must know who I am to petition. Or fight."

She bristled. How quickly his emotions turned to business and bloodshed.

"You seem certain of my brother's arrival." She wished she could be so steadfast.

Eliab's stare was as sharp as a flint knife. "If someone snatched my sisters, I would hunt them down like a froth-mouthed animal."

"Nadab." The name stuck in Naomi's throat. "Nadab is the only sibling I have left."

"Then I hope he is evenhanded." Eliab trudged on, not realizing the heaviness he had placed upon her heart.

"And your sisters? How were they named?"

Would Eliab reveal the names of the dead? A shiver traveled down her back. Had she gone too far in effort to find peace, a bond, some respect?

The shuffling of hooves answered her inquest.

"Dorcas and Deborah." Eliab breathed their names with a reverence that struck her speechless. "My mother carried another child when she was slain."

Naomi's heart sank deep in her chest. What could be said to heal such a wound? Enough words had been spoken. Enough words about Gibeah and war. *Find me, Nadab. Find me soon.*

As twilight fell, a structure came into view. Eliab's pace quickened. She stumbled in trying to keep up with his long strides. At least she would have shelter this night. If Berek was a lawful leader, he would respect her heritage and see she was treated with dignity. She needed a reprieve until Ephraim came for justice.

The scrape of Eliab's sandals across barren soil reminded Naomi of Cuzbi's boasts of rich lands and much wealth on the first night of their capture. These fields held no crops or livestock. Not a servant was in sight to fodder the mule or wash their feet. Whatever Ashbanel told Cuzbi about the riches of Berek had all been a lie. Poor Cuzbi. She would find her friend and console her.

Eliab tied the mule to a fence outside a courtyard. The splintered wood was held together with strips of leather. Even in a time of mourning, Eliab and his family had built a house and a stable with an upper room. Divots in the stone contained soot from the fires of condemnation. The windows looked like empty sockets without an eyeball or lash, without linen or drape.

Braying began. Eliab stroked the mule's muzzle. "Now he complains. When he is home."

The door to the house burst open. Ashbanel stomped across the courtyard.

Naomi stepped backward, using Eliab as a shield. She had already been questioned by Ashbanel. And once was enough.

"Where have you been?" Ashbanel prodded Eliab in the chest. "Father is distraught. You did not arrive with the group."

Pivoting, Eliab avoided another poke. "I was detained. We met up with some Moabites—"

"Detained."

Ashbanel's roar sent a cold stream through Naomi's veins.

"The only thing that should have detained you shouldn't have taken very long." Ashbanel scrutinized her like he was stitching together the seams at every curve of her body.

She shuddered and crossed her arms over her breasts.

"I took charge of Isa." Eliab growled his excuse. "You left him behind."

"And Jael," Naomi added in Eliab's defense.

Ashbanel lunged around Eliab and grabbed Naomi's wrist, tugging her forward.

"You dare to address an elder of Benjamin without a bow?"

Her mouth parched. She dangled from Ashbanel's grasp as a slaughtered goat hung to bleed.

Eliab stepped nose to nose with his brother. "She will bow. She is weary and misspoke." His rebuff held enough remorse to spare her a strike and gain her release from Ashbanel's clutches.

Naomi crouched to the ground. She clenched her fists into her lap. Oh, how she wanted to lash out at this imposter. What elder robs his fellow Israelites of their daughters in the dark of night? She stayed low until she felt a hand upon her back. Eliab lifted her to her feet as if she were crafted of fine alabaster.

"*Shalom,*" she whispered. She retreated to Eliab's side and did not cower from Ashbanel's scowl.

"Naomi." The shriek came from the courtyard. Cuzbi dashed toward her, arms open, her robe billowing.

Naomi scrambled toward Cuzbi and embraced her friend. "Praise God you are safe." Naomi's resolve strengthened from the familiar hug. "Stay strong, sister." Naomi spoke softly. "Our rescuers will be here soon. Your father will have scouts all over Gibeah."

"My father." Cuzbi giggled. The faintest odor of sour wine filled the air between their faces. "Silly Naomi, why would I want my father to find me?" Cuzbi swaggered in an attempt to talk into Naomi's ear. "I am no longer a virgin." Her confession, emboldened by too much drink, carried into the night.

"This cannot be." Naomi's knee joints threatened to give way. Had Cuzbi turned her back on the tribe of Ephraim? "He filled you with wine."

"Not the second time." Cuzbi's voice reverberated through the courtyard. "Or the third."

Ashbanel slapped Eliab on the back. "The line of Berek shall have an heir."

Eliab stroked his jaw, disguising a grin, but Naomi could not tell if it was a smirk of anticipation for what was to come tonight or amusement at Cuzbi's carefree demeanor.

Naomi's skin tingled as if Eliab had reached out

and brushed her flesh with his fingertips. Her pulse hammered a warning through her temples.

You. Are. Next.

8

Naomi stood anchored to the dirt, desperate and alone like a leper banished from the walls of a city. Where were her tribesmen? She would need all her wits to keep her virginity intact until they arrived. Would Eliab be a man of reason?

Cuzbi turned and staggered toward the open door.

She grasped Cuzbi's shoulder to help her stay upright. No gold glimmered on her friend's hand. Cuzbi's fingers were bare. Heat flashed through Naomi's body. "Where are your rings and headband?"

"My husband is keeping them safe." Cuzbi slurred as if her tongue had thickened. "We stopped in Op…opra…rah to barter."

Naomi supported Cuzbi's weight and propelled her toward the house of Berek and away from Ashbanel. "Don't you see? Ashbanel has deceived you." Naomi kept her voice low, but it rasped with desperation. "There is no wealth here. No fertile fields. No servants. We will serve these Benjamites as slaves or worse."

Cuzbi's forehead ridged. "My husband will succeed Berek. He is the eldest son. There is plenty of land here." Cuzbi flung her arm. "You know how to work the soil and there is a shepherd boy living nearby to tend the flocks."

"What will you tell your father when he comes?" She steadied Cuzbi's sway. How could she get her friend to see the barrenness?

"Unlike Heriah, my father does not need to sell me to prosper. Can't your husband scrounge something of value to satisfy your family? I am not waiting any longer to be someone's wife." Cuzbi swiped her tongue across her teeth. "You are a laborer's daughter. Uncover that man's feet and slip into his bed. For what man in Ephraim will offer for you since you have nestled in a Benjamite's lap?"

Naomi's cheeks flamed. These were not the words of her friend. The wine spoke this gibberish. "I will not leap into Eliab's bed."

"Why not? He is handsome. At least here you will own the land instead of toil upon it," Cuzbi said, brushing her off like a loose thread.

Naomi trembled with rage. "And what of their evil ways?"

"The war is over, Naomi. Look to the future and not the past." Cuzbi grabbed the faded wood of the doorway and shuffled inside the house.

"And how many brothers did you lose in battle?" Naomi knew the answer. None.

An elderly man dodged by Cuzbi and rushed from the doorway without a glance or a nod in Naomi's direction. His beard was as full as his turban. This had to be Berek, Eliab's father and renegade elder of Benjamin.

"Eliab, my son, you have returned."

None other.

Berek pressed his hands to Eliab's face and stared as if he had not seen his son in months.

After a moment, Eliab withdrew from his father. "I am home with a wife." Eliab hurried toward Naomi.

Should she fall at Berek's feet and beg for a

release? She leaned against the doorpost, contemplating her plea. Her countenance fell. If Berek was set upon a grandchild from her womb, why would he honor a request for mercy?

"This is Naomi *bat* Heriah of Shiloh." Eliab strode forward and pried her from the doorframe. He escorted her to his father as if she were a gift.

Naomi lowered to one knee, but the mention of her father's name caused her chest to constrict with pride and grief. A longing for her family built behind her eyes. She stifled her shuddered breaths, vying for Berek's favor.

"Welcome, my daughter. *Shalom.* We shall celebrate your arrival. God has returned my sons to me and provided wives to produce many children." Berek motioned for her to rise. His gaze swept from the crown of her head to her dusty toes.

"*Shalom*—" Her throat seized. She could not bring herself to call this man father. Nodding, she gave a brief smile. How could this elder thank the God whose laws he refused to uphold among his people? Had Berek not allowed idol worship in Gibeah? She drew closer to Eliab.

"We will celebrate tomorrow," Eliab said. "Our trip was delayed by Moabite thieves."

"Even our enemies come to pick at the remains of Benjamin." Berek urged them inside the house. "Surely a drink is needed after such a journey."

Wine would not touch her lips until she was safely in Shiloh. Then she would celebrate.

"Perhaps one." Eliab halted inside the doorway.

She clasped her hands and inspected Eliab's home. The furnishings fared no better than a prisoner's cell. Mats adorned the floor, plain mats, with no ornate weave. A few uncarved chairs angled in the corner. How could Cuzbi not see the poverty before her? The tribes of Israel had devastated Benjamin. Their own people were responsible for this barrenness.

"Wash your feet and join us." Ashbanel reclined at a table littered with wooden plates and cups. Cuzbi clung to Ashbanel as a bride enjoying her weeklong marriage festivities.

Berek joined his eldest son at the table and, tipping his drink, seemed to offer a toast to her arrival.

Eliab cleared his throat. He sat by the door near the washbasin.

Naomi beheld the black night through the open doorway. What lay beyond, should she choose to escape? Did Gera linger nearby? Or another foreigner in need of a slave or wife? Her lips quivered. *I want to be in Shiloh, not East Gibeah.*

"Naomi." Eliab's voice shattered her trance. He held up a cloth. "Wash me and I will wash you."

Kneeling, she dipped the rag and listened to the familiar slosh of water. Living in a home full of field workers, she had wiped clean many a foot, but she feared Eliab desired more than a foot washing. Would her touch kindle a roaring lust? Her insides fluttered as though a bat were caged inside her body. *I am not ready. I need time.*

Her father may not have owned a booth in the market, but she had learned how to barter with her brothers. If they returned home too tired or drunk to finish their work, she would offer to do their chores for a price. Perhaps with all her trading skills, she could persuade Eliab to delay their marriage bed.

She took extra care to massage in between each one of Eliab's toes. He sank into the chair with his eyes lidded as she swept the cloth around his heel and along the length of his arch. His relaxed state increased her boldness. Her stomach squirmed, for she knew the measure of what she was about to ask.

"If I allow you to clean my feet," she whispered, thumbs gently caressing his skin, "will you keep me clean until the Sabbath?"

Eliab's eyes opened slowly as if he was deciphering her request. No humor graced his expression. "That is three and a half days."

"In a lifetime, it is but a blink." She dried his feet and avoided his scrutinizing stare.

He removed the rag from her hands. "You're letting me touch you now."

As she sat, mischief awakened in his eyes. Her heart skittered as he grasped her foot. Was he in agreement to her request? She wrapped her hem around her legs so only her feet dipped in the water. "You may wash below my ankles."

Ashbanel scowled as Eliab lowered himself to the floor in front of her.

Eliab stroked her arches with enough power to rattle her composure. She clung to the chair and stifled a reprimand. Her stomach rolled like a boat tossed on a stormy sea.

She bent in close. "That is all I need." She gritted her teeth so as not to cry out from the tickle.

He put his face next to her ear. His stubble bristled against her cheek. "It is not all I need if I am going to wait for you."

Her breaths hitched as he caressed her toes. Leaning forward and placing a hand on each side of his face, she drew him close.

"Please stop. My insides are jumping like a flea.

Say you'll agree to wait, for I am an orphan with no one to petition in my favor. I have already shamed myself once this day. Do not make me dishonor myself again."

"Hurry up," Ashbanel grunted. "Was the grove not enough for you?"

Eliab flinched and turned toward his brother. "What do you know of the grove?" His tone was bitter as a wild herb.

Naomi stiffened. Had she offended Eliab with her request? Certainly he would keep the lie of their false union.

"Gera ranted to me about your betrayal." Ashbanel swallowed a mouthful of bread. "He believes you stole his dancer. He wanted his grievance heard by an elder."

Naomi started a defense, but then remembered Ashbanel's harsh reprimand upon their arrival.

Eliab handed her a towel and crossed to the table in a few strides. Hands on his hips, Eliab dwarfed the room. "I did not take Naomi from Gera. She came to me. Does the Lord not answer the prayers of the downtrodden?"

"I believe He does." Berek motioned for his son to sit by his side. "The girl is yours, Eliab. Gera is jealous. God did not see fit to provide a wife for him."

Ashbanel popped an olive in his mouth. "From the look of it, he has spouted lies that are of no consequence. The man brings up too much of the past." Ashbanel gave Eliab a knowing look.

"The past is dead," Eliab said. "And you know the truth."

Naomi clutched the towel to her chest. The cloth quaked from the boom of her heart. Why was Gera making these allegations? Had he not been convinced in the grove that Eliab had taken her as his wife? And if he found out she was still a virgin, would he claim her and take her from Eliab?

"It has been a long trip." Eliab kissed his father's hand. "I am going to take my wife to bed." Eliab's statement rang with a renewed fervor. His emphasis of the last word caused her legs to go limp.

Was Eliab worried about Gera's accusations? Would Eliab honor her request to wait? Or would her belly be the next to bulge with a Benjamite baby?

9

Slowly, with a lack of haste, Naomi ascended the stepladder to Eliab's bedroom above the stable. Her heart rate spiked with every footfall, for Eliab had not agreed to wait on a union. She followed her abductor, but stayed in the doorway, shifting her weight from sandal to sandal, contemplating a retreat into the darkness. But where would she run? And who was lurking outside the courtyard walls? Gera or another Benjamite bent on claiming a wife?

Eliab crossed the room and emptied a waterskin into a bowl. "I must cleanse myself. I have been gone for days." He threw off his tunic.

She covered her eyes.

Eliab chuckled. "Surely you have seen a bare-chested man in the fields. I did not remove my loincloth."

"Seeing laborers in the vineyard is different. I keep my distance and there are people about. I am not accustomed to having a stranger disrobe a stone's roll from where I stand. Let alone when I am near where he sleeps."

"I am not a stranger." A hint of frustration strangled his defense.

"We've known each other a few days. There has been no betrothal period. No consent from my father." She removed her hands from her face and averted her gaze while shuffling along the farthest wall. "I need more time. Will you agree to my petition to wait until the Sabbath?"

"Only if you agree to my request."

"You did not make one."

What would he require of her?

Eliab wrapped a cloth around his hips but did not seem in a hurry to dry or cover his chest. "I am making one now. If I am to control myself until after the Sabbath, then you must accompany me wherever I go during our brief betrothal."

"Everywhere?" Her voice squeaked as she envisioned the worst possible places to accompany a man.

"Within reason." He spoke as if this was an ordinary deal witnessed at the city gate. "I do not want you seized when my back is turned."

"By Gera?" Even speaking his name sent a cool stream of water down her spine.

"By anyone." Eliab's voice hovered above a whisper. "We are not yet joined as one."

"I do not want to be like Cuzbi." The shock of her friend's revelation weighed her down like an overflowing water jar. No ceremony had taken place in the presence of Cuzbi's family. The traditions of their people had been cast off because of the needs of one tribe.

"I gathered that by your reaction earlier." Eliab drew closer and lay on his back on a sleeping mat in the middle of the floor. A blanket lay in a mound at his feet. He grimaced as he stretched. "Come and sleep."

"Aren't you going to wear a tunic?"

"I believe a loincloth will be plenty warm." He patted the space beside him.

She inched forward. Her ears and brain buzzed

with the haunting echo of a ram's horn blast. Would Eliab be able to resist the temptation of lying next to a woman, chest to breast, leg to thigh? "I am in agreement if you are."

"Mm-hmm." Eliab's response rumbled from his throat.

She reclined by his side, picturing a barricade between their bodies. Instead of donkey dander, the scent of cassia and cloves filled the air. Had he put herbs in the basin in case he captured a dancer? Removing her veil, she tucked the cloth underneath her head, but she could not ignore the shape beside her. Her breathing quickened. Too fast. Too shallow. Her lungs began to burn. Eliab rolled onto his side, dwarfing her imaginary wall. His hair fell around his shoulders and he beheld her with sleepy eyes. Cuzbi spoke the truth. He was handsome. The weeks spent rebuilding his home and his city had left him broader than most of the laborers she had seen in the vineyards. One smothering embrace from him and she would be engulfed into that hard chest. No. No. No. She rubbed her arms to distract her thoughts.

"You are restless," he said, propping his head upon his elbow.

"I am accustomed to sleeping with my mother." And not accustomed to such a thin, poorly woven mat. She licked her cracked lips, but her tongue was a dried reed. "You have ridden that donkey for days. Settle down. I will not disturb you."

"On my back, thieves could hold me down and slit my throat. Staying on my side, I am ready to do battle." He lowered himself so his face became even with hers.

"There is nothing of value here." The upper room

held only a bed, a washbasin, and candle wax.

"Oh yes, there is. There is something priceless here." His dark brown eyes glimmered as if he slept next to rows of gold coins. "But she is safe with me."

"Even from Gera? He is furious with—" Eliab's finger touched her lip and lingered. His skin had softened from the washing.

She shivered at his intimate caress, and when he removed his hand, the warmth of his touch remained upon her lip.

"He is brazen if he thinks he can plot against the house of Berek. Ashbanel was a fool to have married Gera's sister." Eliab's arm rested upon her waist.

Her belly jumped as if she had swallowed a locust, but she did not protest. In his cocoon of strength, she found a moment of refuge.

"Gera's kin mocked the Law and our prophets. They worshipped idols, and their perverse petitions to false gods overflowed into the streets. They have the blood of the Levite's wife on their hands. I am blameless, as is the line of Berek." His stare fixed on her face. "Do you believe I am innocent?"

She did. She had to. With him, she had a measure of hope. Hope for protection. Hope for a rescue. Hope that God would not abandon the girls of Shiloh.

"Yes, I believe you," she whispered. "I am thankful you have honored my request."

"I have not slept in days. When we come together again, I may regret my decision."

"But you will still honor it?"

He leaned closer and brushed a loose ringlet behind her ear. His breath bathed her cheek.

She became sculpture-still.

"Until after the Sabbath. Yes." His hand grazed the

contour of her cheek. "Now rest, Naomi." The length of his arm cradled her hips.

Was this an innocent display of protection? A snare if she tried to flee? She wanted to find rest, but a riptide of emotions rallied her conscience for battle.

Her chest tightened. If she returned to Shiloh, Eliab would have no wife or children. A sprig from the vine of Jacob and Rachel would wither. She didn't want to be a traitor to the memory of her brothers. They fought with valor to uphold God's laws. Where did she belong? Her spirit was torn. She wished for a sign, for she ached to see her family. *What is my future, Lord?* Was she to help the wayward tribe of Benjamin survive? Or curse Eliab's line into extinction?

10

When she awoke, Eliab was gone. He had honored their agreement to keep her chaste. Perhaps an honorable remnant remained in the land of Benjamin. Though today she would keep her distance from her would-be husband and not tempt his self-control.

She washed her face and went outside to bake bread. If she did not eat soon, she would faint from the escalating heat.

Descending the steps from the upper room, she scanned the structures, trying to find her protector. Eliab rounded the corner from the stable with a bridle tucked under his arm.

"*Boker tov.*" His voice rose as if he greeted guests at a party. "You are awake early." He strode toward her, arms extended. Was he going to lift her down to the ground?

She jumped off the last rung before his hands could engulf her waist. "Are you going somewhere?" Better to change the subject and send him back into the stable to finish readying the mule than to have him greet her wholeheartedly.

"We," he began, intimating their collaboration with the rotation of his hand, "are going into the mountains to hunt for livestock. There are more mouths to feed, and we've had to travel far of late to find animals that survived the slaughter. I do not have jewels from my wife to sell."

Was he insulting her lack of wealth? Recalling the theft of Cuzbi's rings awakened hostility inside her soul. Her friend was too easily swayed in thinking Benjamites were more than thieves and scoundrels. She arched her shoulders and put her hands on her hips. "Would you sell them if you did?"

"I have been able to provide for my family without a woman's trinkets." Eliab looped the reins around his arm. "And today we'll have an extra scout."

Good. A chaperone. "Surely separate mounts will make your work easier." Riding in his lap all day might cause him to lust for the night.

He stifled a grin. "Of course. How can I rope and harness with a barrier in front of me?"

Barrier? She wasn't an ox. "If you insist." As she turned away, her belly rumbled. Long and loud. She clutched her robe and tried to quiet the gurgle.

"You will find oil and flour by the fire pit. Hurry and prepare us something to eat so we may be on our way." He backed toward the stable. "Your body sounds like it needs some roasted lamb."

Thoughts of meat on a spit caused her mouth to water and her stomach to churn all the more. She added to the fire in the courtyard, inhaling the familiar scent of ash and charred wood.

When she was almost done cooking the dough on a heated stone, Jael planted herself at Naomi's side. Isa hurried to join Eliab. The boy's hair snaked in every direction as if he had been caught in a windstorm. His wrap barely contained the mass of curls. Jael rubbed a braided leather band that secured her indigo head covering.

"Isa wove this band for me." Jael's broad smile was too bright for the early hour of the morning.

Naomi stroked the weave. "He will have to show me how he tightened the hide without it twisting." She lifted the last piece of manna from the stone and glanced at her friend. "Were you safe last night?" She sucked in a breath and held it, waiting for Jael's answer.

"No drunkards came in the night to pester me. Isa has a small home, but I did not have to knot the ties of my tent as in Shiloh." Jael broke the bread into wafers. "And you fared well?" Jael bit into a burnt corner. Her cheeks reddened as if embarrassed by her boldness.

Naomi tightened the belt around Jael's waist. Should she mention her arrangement with Eliab? Could Jael keep her secret? The girl seemed to be growing fond of Isa. What if Jael blurted the truth? She needed to protect herself and Jael.

"I still owe you a garment, and I would have had plenty of time to set a loom last night as Eliab snored till dawn."

"Will we find thread here?" Jael rocked forward and threw a branch on the graying embers.

"I doubt any survived the fires. Perhaps I will come across a village on the trails today."

"You are accompanying the men?" Jael's eyes widened.

"At Eliab's request." She grabbed hold of Jael's arms and felt a tremor. "You will be safe. Eliab's father and brother are elders. They must protect a daughter of Israel." She doubted Isa had recounted the abuse of the Levite's wife to Jael. Naomi shuddered at the memory. "A long trip into the hills may take all day. Do not worry." She fingered Jael's band. "With a gift like this, Isa cares for your well-being." And with Isa along, there was a better chance of her own well-being.

Eliab and Isa joined them in the courtyard and consumed Naomi's bread as if she had offered them raisin cakes and honey. Isa stationed himself beside Jael and left a hand upon her back while Eliab stocked provisions on their mules.

Jael accepted Isa's caress without a flinch. Was Jael growing fond of her captor in the same way as Cuzbi? *Am I alone in my disdain?*

Naomi wrapped the remaining bread in linen and hurried toward her mule. Oh, to be on the trail, alone on her mount. A thought sprang to her lips. "Shall we pray for a blessing before our journey?"

"I'm not singing this time." Isa brushed off his tunic and knelt to the north, toward Bethel, where the Lord had revealed Himself to their ancestor Jacob.

"A blessing would be nice instead of a curse." Eliab bowed low. He cleared his throat. "Hear, O Israel. The Lord our God, the Lord is one. May we find favor in Your eyes today, O God." He cocked his head and looked her direction.

Their eyes met. Had she been staring at him through prayer? She shut her eyes and spoke the petition anew, willing her cheeks not to flame scarlet.

"*Selah*." Eliab spoke the benediction above her crouched body.

She remained tucked in a bow, taking a few moments to revel in the firmness of the soil beneath her forehead and the warmth of the ground beneath her palms. Just her. In solitude. She needed strength to last another day.

"It is time to leave." Eliab drew her to her feet.

They approached the mules. Hers did not have a waterskin. Did Eliab expect her to flee? Did their vow not give him a sense of peace?

Hours later, the sun showed little mercy as they labored up paths no wider than the mules' shoulders. Even when Naomi squinted, the terrain remained whitewashed. Shadows evaporated underneath the day's harsh glare. The top of her head warmed hotter than a silversmith's fire.

How did Eliab find his way? A sea of rocks, large, small, jagged, worn, walled her in a desolate mirage. She clung to her mule, every muscle taut. The animal navigated narrow ridges without a glance toward the deep drops. Her eyes shut the moment pebbles cascaded off the side of the path.

"This is treacherous." Voicing the danger knotted her stomach.

Eliab twisted and caught her attention. "So is not eating. Fear not—the mule is sure-footed."

Isa tossed a grape in the air and caught it with his mouth. "Eliab," he called, throwing a grape at their leader. Eliab caught it faster than a snapping turtle.

"Naomi."

Before she knew what was happening, an object pelted her in the nose and fell to the ground. Of all the childish games! Staying balanced on the uneven trail was task enough, let alone leaning off the side of a mule. "'Tis a waste," she scolded.

"Not if you catch it." Isa chomped on another grape. His cheeks puffed as if he had stuffed an entire cluster in his mouth. "Did we not meet these girls in a vineyard?"

Meet? Did he jest?

Eliab stifled a laugh. "Give her a warning. They may not be as quick in Shiloh."

Another grape tapped her cheek and plunged to the dirt.

She envisioned flinging something harder than a grape at their cackling faces. She sat straighter. "You did not call my name."

"Naomi," Eliab blurted out.

Humiliation would come swiftly if she missed the next grape. Opening her mouth, she thrust herself forward and bit down. Sweet, watery syrup soothed her tongue. A victory.

Isa clapped.

She wiped her mouth. "Ephraim is not without honor."

Eliab shushed their banter. "Listen."

"For what?" Isa slumped. "We have scouted this ravine before and not found a stray."

Holding up one hand, Eliab motioned with his other.

Naomi heard a faint bleating. Was she imagining the muffled protest?

Isa shot up, his back straight as an axle. "I hear it too. What are you waiting for? Someone to steal our sheep?"

Eliab kicked his mule and crested the hill.

She and Isa gave chase.

Naomi gasped. A herd of ewes, a ram, and a kid huddled in the basin of a wadi as if waiting to be sheared.

Eliab splayed his arms wide. "The God of Abraham, Isaac, and Jacob heard our prayers. Look what He has provided."

"These have to be from someone's herd. A caravan's." Isa surveyed the hills for a shepherd.

"They're ours. Look." Eliab indicated a barricade of jumbled rock. "A landslide has trapped our blessing. God is smiling on Benjamin." Eliab dismounted, passed by Isa, and whisked Naomi off her mule. "Sometimes we searched for days and only found a small coney."

Her stomach swirled as Eliab lifted her high into the air. She hovered for a moment, gazing into his jubilant face. Suddenly, he lowered her and plunged into a mouth-crushing kiss. Her bones became like dust in his embrace. How long did a kiss last? Her pent-up breath ached to be released. She jabbed his chest.

He drew back.

As their lips parted, her mouth hung open. The tingle from his kiss dropped an anchor to her toes. She wrapped her arms around her waist to stop the sensation sprouting behind her navel. "You promised you would wait." Her face flushed, for the press of his body still lingered on her chest.

"It was a celebratory kiss. Certainly you've had one before?" He watched her like a spy, noting her reaction. He knew. He had to know. His kiss was not unpleasant.

"I have had no such celebrations." Her reply did not hold the harsh rebuke she intended.

"You trust me in the dark, yet not in the daylight?" A slaked-thirst grin eclipsed his face while he stroked her cheek. "We do have company." He motioned toward Isa, whose elation focused on their bounty.

"Perhaps you should see to the animals." Her cadence rose and fell as she struggled for composure.

Eliab strolled toward Isa, but before he joined his partner, he glanced back and gave her a look her father would have forbidden.

Her insides twisted, but not in an unpleasant fashion, more as if someone tickled her gut with a strip of cloth. She fisted her hand and pressed it harder and harder against her belly until the sensation ceased.

Her plan to keep Eliab at a distance had failed. Tonight she would give every reason not to share his bed. She believed him trustworthy and did not question his word, nor did she question his honor, but he was an unwed man in haste for a child. And at this moment, she questioned her traitorous body more than she questioned him.

11

Naomi trailed after Eliab, keeping a respectable distance as he inspected the livestock trapped in the basin. She treaded lightly on the path, grateful that it widened so she did not have to hover near the worn-rock sides of the ravine. Was this provision from God her sign to remain with Eliab?

Isa shouted and clicked his tongue, sending commands to the herd. A few sheep angled toward his call. He squatted on the ridge and motioned to the ewes to come closer. "I believe some of these are ours. They know my voice."

"How are we to get them out?" Naomi inched forward to see if hoof holds jutted from the sides of the wadi. None did. At some point, water had ground the stone smooth like a pestle. Surveying the drop made her feet unsteady. Her temples throbbed. She slowly sidestepped from the edge.

Eliab took hold of her arm. His shadow gave her shade. "We will harness the sheep and lift them up the slope. Then we will herd them down the trails."

"We'd better hurry." Isa grabbed a rope from his mount and came toward her, slip-knotting a loop. "The whining of the herd will alert predators."

Was Isa going to rope her like a goat? She tensed for a struggle.

Eliab blocked Isa's path. "She cannot go down and wrestle livestock."

Should she confess she had shoved stubborn goats out of the vineyards? Or continue to allow Eliab to act as her husband? Crossing her arms, she waited for a settlement or a fight.

Isa snapped the rope in protest. "The animals will be tied. How much of a fight will it be?" He cocked his head. "If she cannot herd them or bind them, why did you bring her along?"

Surely Eliab would not discuss their agreement.

Eliab bent over Isa as if he chastised a son. "What if she is with child?" He raised an eyebrow, daring Isa to dispute his claim.

Naomi cast her glance anywhere but at Isa. When would the lies end?

"She is not a feather. She's a laborer's daughter."

In the land of Benjamin, she needed allies, not enemies, especially a lethal left-handed slinger. Isa had accompanied Ashbanel and Berek when they fled the war. She did not need Isa complaining to Berek about Eliab's actions. She already had Gera petitioning a wife from Ashbanel.

She stepped toward Isa and looked back at Eliab, meeting his scowl. "I know to be careful of the ram's horns. It will be far less strenuous than shearing the sheep. I am not afraid to handle livestock." She smiled at Eliab and gave his shoulder a reassuring pat. At least he would be kept at a distance. No more unexpected kisses.

Eliab snatched the coil from Isa. "I will secure her." Leaning in close, he hesitated to cinch her waist. "You do not need to go down there."

"Isa has been a friend to the household of Berek. He asks for little, and we do need to eat. God has provided the abundance. Now we'll ask for protection."

"If you are sure." He eased the loop over her head and down to her hips. "Tell me at once if you are hurt." The seriousness of his concern contrasted with his harsh binding of her in the grove.

She grasped the rope and scaled the embankment toe to heel. She did not gaze at the drop, but remained intent on the faces of the men above. Eliab kept the rope taut, securing the line around the girth of a boulder while Isa weighted the end. When he shuffled his feet, small dirt clods dislodged. She averted her stare. For a moment. A brief moment.

"You are almost there." Eliab encouraged her to keep a steady rhythm.

"*Selah*. Praise God," she said as her sandals landed on solid ground.

With a keen eye, she surveyed the sheep milling around the displaced rock. An avalanche of dirt and stone prevented a retreat.

"Scare the fat ewe in our direction." Isa pointed to a sheep in the rear of the herd. "The docile ones will be easier to corral. We will finish sooner."

Naomi raced toward the sheep, clapping and chasing the stragglers toward Eliab and Isa. Instantly, Eliab lassoed the animal's neck. The sheep bucked. Isa landed a coil of rope near the animal's legs. She wrestled the hind legs into Isa's noose and shifted the rope to the underbelly. Whisked up into the air, the beast bleated its displeasure. One down and only two small hoof scratches on her forearm.

Eliab cupped his hands around his mouth. "Do you need a rest?"

Perspiration snaked down the side of her face. *No.* No rest. No time for him to charm her and sneak another kiss. As soon as the livestock were captured, Eliab would be distracted with the herd, caring for their thirst, hunger, and safety. A simple but true claim of exhaustion from her labors kept her safe in his bed another night. "Which one next?"

Eliab indicated a grazing sheep.

Naomi pursued the animals, sending them into Eliab's snares. The lone ram defied her long-stick prodding, but she'd riled him enough to charge her. She ran toward the side of the wadi, and the ram almost made it to her backside before he was brought down. Panting heavily, she said a prayer of thanks for the Benjamites' precision.

A young goat hovered at the far end of the ravine. Did he sense her intentions or was he spooked by the commotion of the harnessing? Naomi straightened her skirt and angled its direction.

Movement caught her attention as she passed a station of boulders. A pathetic *eh-eh-eh* erupted from among the jumbled stone. A ewe struggled, her hind legs crushed by the cut-loose cliff.

Naomi crouched low and examined the female. "You are carrying a lamb." She stroked its wide belly, removing pebbles and dirt from its coat. The mother turned a concerned eye but didn't challenge Naomi's touch.

"Naomi. Are you lost?" Eliab's shout rang out from the ridge with more volume than before. Did he think she grew faint?

"I am here." She stood and waved her hand. "I have found another ewe."

Isa hooted. "Chase it toward us."

"I cannot. She is lame."

Eliab readied his rope. "Leave it and get the goat."

"She will labor soon." Naomi's chest grew heavy as if she was bundled by a harness. How could she leave the mother and baby to die? "Please, Eliab. I will run after the goat, but I want to take this ewe."

"How?" Isa grunted, wrestling the ram from the edge of the ravine. "We have all we can handle."

"Isa is correct." Eliab readied his lasso without looking her direction. "See to the other one."

"Must I?" Her eyes tingled with tears as if she had raced into a sandstorm. "I do not want to leave this mother to toil away as her baby dies within her."

"Wife, do my bidding." Eliab's command sharpened.

Isa paced near the rescued herd.

She stormed closer to the incline. "Did we not ask God to provide? He has chosen to give us sickness along with health. What if this is a test of our faith?"

"It is a test of my patience." Isa took aim at her with his rope.

Naomi scurried backward, her eyes on Isa's aim.

Eliab grabbed the boy's arm and knocked him off balance.

Had her testimony swayed him? "I will carry her, Eliab. Place me on the mule and she can rest in my lap."

"This is folly," Isa shouted. "She will slow us down. Let us finish the task at hand and be done."

"Let it be my gift." The excuse fled from her lips. "Jael received a present this morning." Her heart drummed. She hoped Eliab would not resent the comparison to a boy or think her jealous. Either way, it didn't matter. She wouldn't leave the ewe to suffer alone.

Eliab scratched his stubbled jaw and glanced at

Isa. "Is this true?"

Isa shrugged. "The girl needed a band, so I wove one. It made her happy and she slept."

"So I have you to blame." Eliab rested a coil of rope on his hip.

"The girl is your burden, not mine." Isa pointed her direction. "I have one of my own."

"Make haste with the goat," Eliab called to her. "If you can carry the ewe within our range, we will bring it home."

With renewed energy, she charged the goat. It bolted behind her, straight toward Eliab, who had his lasso at the ready. The goat balked at the cord around its neck, but she grasped its hindquarters and forced it into the second harness.

She rested for a moment. "I believe I earned my gift. I have never had to fight with a cluster of grapes."

Eliab laughed. "Hurry and claim the ewe before Isa runs off with our bounty."

She rushed to the boulders and scattered the rubble to get ahold of the breeding ewe. The animal trembled in her arms as she lifted it from the scattered stones. Naomi held her breath and counted her steps, willing herself not to drop the sheep.

Isa shook his head while he pulled the ewe to the top of the ridge. "This is madness."

Eliab tossed her the rope. "I can see to Naomi and her *gift* if you want to start the herd home. Unless you need my help?" Eliab gave Isa a raised-eyebrow challenge.

"Hah. With this lot? We will be in East Gibeah before you mount." Isa prodded the restless herd toward his mule. "Mind the goat yourself. That animal is possessed. I do not want it chasing our bounty over the ledge."

"Nor do I, for I am finished chasing animals today." She massaged her shoulders before her last climb.

Frayed rope sizzled upon her palms as she ascended the side of the ravine. Her muscles bulged as she grabbed hold, pulled, and recaptured the rope. Eliab tugged in rhythm so her footing would not falter.

She slumped to the ground at the top of the ridge. "I hope Jael and Cuzbi have prepared a feast for us so I can rest."

"You are delusional from your labors." Eliab grinned and offered her the waterskin.

"Perhaps. But I can dream." She drank and then let the ewe lap at some water.

Eliab placed their provisions on his mule and then helped her mount. He hesitated before lifting the ewe onto her lap.

"I didn't know you wanted anything from me." His hand rested on hers. "Surely I could have found something more worthy than injured livestock."

She struggled with a reply. At that moment, Eliab seemed vulnerable. A man desperate to make a bad situation better. He had acted honorably toward her and kept her a virgin, but this gift was sought to ease her conscience, not because she had decided to become his wife.

"I don't know what I desire." She met his gaze, but she could tell her truth was not what he expected. Should she be more forthright? Should she reveal that something, some feeling, was beginning to take hold of her? She almost told him that she cared about his future. That his lineage would be a blessing to the tribe of Benjamin. To Israel. But her compliment went unspoken. How could she speak of fondness for a Benjamite when her brothers' bodies lay buried near Gibeah? Where was God's protection for the daughters of Ephraim?

The ewe stirred and grazed Naomi's thigh with its hoof. Consoling the mother during their trip home would be a grand task. She cradled the animal's weight as her mule trotted after Eliab's mount.

Balking at its tether, the young goat made a game of ramming the hind legs of Eliab's mule. The mule kicked in displeasure and sent pebbles cascading over the edge of the trail. Isa was right to leave the beast behind. When the path widened, the goat snarled itself in a bramble bush.

Eliab jumped from his mount. "I am tempted to set this one free." He untangled the animal, and before he renewed his handhold, it charged down the path. "I may have to tuck that menace under my arm." His sandals pounded the baked dirt as he hurried to catch the wayward goat.

When she turned to watch Eliab's pursuit, a sound like the rush of waves filled the air. Pathway disintegrated before her eyes. Soil cascaded down the cliff like a waterfall. Her mule stutter-stepped sideways. Tightening the reins, she grabbed hold of the mane and attempted to secure the ewe with her chest.

She glanced backward. Eliab and the pesky goat were nowhere in sight. A cloud of dust hovered in the spot she had seen them last.

Particles of dirt swarmed her nostrils. "Eliab?" She practically coughed out his name.

No response.

Bellowing again, she waited for an answer.

None came forth.

12

Naomi covered her mouth and stifled a scream. Her hand shook, tapping her nose and cheeks. Would more path collapse? Her face grew hot. Blinking, she squinted through the haze of dust clouding the air. Tears trickled down her cheeks. Why would God allow a tragedy after an afternoon of blessing? Was not Eliab a son of Abraham? Had he not prayed for God's provision and received it?

"Eliab?" Her voice rasped through her suddenly reed-thin throat. She beckoned again, in soothing tones so as not to frighten the mules. *Please answer me.* She had kept Eliab at a distance, hoping for a chance to sort out her future, but she did not want him taken from her altogether. Surely not taken from this life. Where would she find another Benjamite willing to wait and postpone the marriage bed?

"God, I am confused," she mumbled. "Am I to leave? I have a mount and water, but where do I go? I am lost in these hills. Only Eliab knows the way." The ewe gave a soft bleat as a chorus to her prayer. She petted her gift and came forth with a hand full of fur. "Please spare Eliab's life. If you want me to speak truth, I will." Her heart swelled and rallied against her ribs. "I am fond of him."

Clutching the ewe tight, she jumped from the mule and forced herself to fall on her side and avoid crushing her gift. Air rushed from her lungs as her shoulder struck hard ground. She knelt while pain ricocheted down the length of her arm. Settling the ewe off the trail, she secured the mules and eased along the cliff with her back to the jagged rock. Closer and closer she inched to where Eliab had fallen. Her prayers for a rescue would be in vain if Eliab perished, for Gera would snatch her from Berek's door.

Flat to the ground, she crawled near the path's edge. "Lord, I am doing what is good and right in Your sight. May it go well with me as You have promised." She peered to see if Eliab had survived.

Several yards below her, he lay sprawled on a ledge. A blanket of rocks covered him from neck to feet. Blood covered his face, but she did not see a stream of scarlet beneath the stones. His eyes, closed and still, did not flutter in response to her calls. Had death taken him? She spoke his name again. Nothing. Tiny bumps spread like a rash over her arms.

"Lord, do not abandon me in these hills. I need Eliab."

A remembrance came to mind of her father dousing her brothers after they had drunk too much wine. She retraced her steps to Eliab's mount and untied the waterskin. Praying no more soil would crumble underfoot, she dragged herself to the trail's edge and tipped the skin.

Water puddled beside Eliab's cheek and splashed over his face. He flinched. Debris slid from his chest and a groan rumbled forth.

Her chest sank into the loosened soil. "Thank You, Adonai. He lives."

She rained more water onto Eliab, flooding his mouth.

His eyes flew open. Sputtering, he started to rise.

"Don't move," she called out. "You're on a ledge."

Eliab's stare fixed on her as if she were a seraph. "Where—" He choked as he started to speak.

She reached out a hand to stop his movement. "Stay still. The ground gave way when you chased the goat. It is your turn to be roped." She tried to encourage him with a smile, but her lips quivered, and she feared her grin seemed more like a grimace.

His head turned slowly as he assessed his circumstance. "You're here." His words were spoken softly as if by a dying man.

"Yes, yes, I am. We must take care of one another. Are we not God's people?" The false cheerfulness in her words rang hollow.

"I do not feel favored by God." As he rolled toward the cliff, an exasperated curse rose toward the clouds. He knelt and clutched at his head. "The land is moving."

She dug her fingernails into the dirt to calm the storm swirling inside her chest. "Eliab. Look at me." Her voice grew firm. "You cannot leave me here alone. You carried me into this wilderness; now return me to East Gibeah." She hoped her chastising would keep him alert, for an image of him plunging to his death would haunt her all of her days.

He struggled to stand, swaying like a cattail caught in the trade winds. "You want to go back?"

"Be still. I am getting the rope."

Hastening light-footed, she secured a line around the mule's neck and tugged the animal closer to the trail's new edge, but not too close. She and Eliab did not need the earth to cave in again. Tossing an end of the rope to Eliab, she said, "Grab hold."

He caught the coil with his left hand. His right arm

hung limp at his side.

"Can you control the mule?" he asked.

She huffed at his question. "I rode all day and wrestled livestock."

"What if you whip the animal to pull my weight and cannot stop?" Eliab secured the rope around his waist. "It will drag me until it tires."

Naomi's stomach heaved at the horrific image. "I will halt the mule. God is with us."

"If God is with us, why am I down here?"

She laughed and the sound struck her as odd. For in her grief-stricken family, she could not remember the last time she had burst forth openly. "Have you not learned to accept the woe with the blessing?" Her chuckle halted as she wondered if Eliab was a blessing.

He groaned, but she thought it was more from her jest than from his pain. "Pull me up."

She mounted Eliab's mule and slapped its rump, all the while bellowing, "Hah!"

The animal lurched forward, then balked at carting Eliab's weight. She used her hand as a whip, lashing out in panic until her palm turned scarlet. The mule bucked. Commands flew from her mouth. Without warning, the load lessened and the mule darted forward, almost tossing her between its ears.

Eliab called for her to stop.

With fists clamped on the reins, she steadied the mule long enough for Eliab to slip from his harness. Her arms throbbed in a fast rhythm from the pulling.

When the mule calmed, she secured it and ran to Eliab's prone body. She turned him over so he rested in her lap, and she patted his cheek until his gaze met hers.

"For a moment," he murmured, "I thought I was

in Abraham's bosom."

"Abraham knows I am a stranger to these hills. He sent you back to lead me home." She removed her head covering and tore a strip to bandage his bloody forehead.

He winced as she knotted the cloth. "You did not leave me?"

"I am no murderer. I would like to rest with our forefathers when my time here is done."

"Is that all?" His stare penetrated her being.

She closed her eyes, not wanting to fall into his hopeful gaze. What did he want her to say? That she rescued him because she cared for him? Because of love? How could she put into words the bond causing her to stay and rescue him? "Is saving your life not enough?" She shook her head. Forcing a smile to comfort him, she swept blood away from his eye and helped lift him to his feet. "Come. We must get you home so I can tend to these gashes."

"You will have plenty of washing to do. There is not a part of me that has not been crushed." He stumbled toward his mule and cursed as he attempted to pull himself onto his mount.

"What is wrong with your arm?"

"I do not believe it is broken, but it has lost strength. At least you do not have to worry about me breaking our vow tonight."

"Get on that mule before I ask the land to swallow you again." She pushed him with all her strength until he sat upright on his ride. Worry about their arrangement had vanished from her mind the moment the avalanche occurred. She was not wringing her hands over where she would sleep. Not at the moment anyway.

Naomi's countenance plummeted when she saw the ewe, eyes open, watching her as she prepared to leave. She grabbed the waterskin and rushed to where the sheep lay. "I cannot manage you both." She cast a glance at Eliab, slumped over the mule's neck. Tears strained against Naomi's eyes as she gave the mother a drink. "I am sorry I offered you hope, for now I cannot give it." She stroked the ewe for the last time. "*Shalom,* mother. May God show you His mercy in death as in life."

The ewe's eyes shut as if she was resigned to her fate. Naomi's heart became a rock in her flesh. How much more could she bear? She pushed all emotion deep inside her chest to the place where she stored the grief of her brothers' passing, the loss of her mother's touch, and the fear of remaining apart from her family forever.

She rushed toward Eliab and rubbed his leg to keep him from teetering off his ride. Tethering the mules together, her fingers fumbled the last knot. She would not look at her ewe again.

"I will carry her. She is your gift." The regret in Eliab's voice caused her throat to seize.

"You are barely able to keep yourself upright, let alone manage livestock with one limp arm. All I ask is that you get us to East Gibeah." She sat behind him and kicked the mule, not wanting to dwell on their distress.

The afternoon sun beat down upon her back as if her bones were kindling. Shielding Eliab from the glare as much as she could, she pressed her arms into his sides to keep him awake. Her scheme to keep their bodies apart had been abandoned. Her drenched robe pressed upon Eliab's body. Heat radiated from his skin and awakened a sensation inside of her that was not disagreeable and far less scary than it had been lying in his bed.

She cast her gaze upon the ground, away from their intertwined bodies, and spied a grape among the pebbles. *Isa.* They were on the correct path and near level ground.

"We are not far from your home." Relief simmered in her statement.

Eliab arched his back. The thread of separation between them cooled her like a dip in the river.

"You doubted me?" he said. "I can do these trails by memory."

"Then they are all yours, for I do not care to remember them."

The mules trotted with vigor when they reached open country. Naomi relaxed, knowing the inclines and steep slopes were behind them.

Riders approached.

"Your family has come to find us." She adjusted her posture, contemplating what to say if questioned about the wounds.

Eliab straightened. "That is not my father, nor my brother."

Her blood chilled as she recognized the wide body on the lead mule. It had to be Gera.

And that perverse man was not alone.

13

Naomi had to get Eliab to East Gibeah, a place where they would both be safe. She steered the mule away from Gera and the band of men riding in his wake. With Eliab's wounds, he could not defend himself, nor her, in a dispute. She tightened her hold on the reins. If anyone came too close, she would lash out. Not one finger would she allow to touch her. Not without injury. She leaned into Eliab's back. He had been her protector, and she would make sure he survived this encounter.

Gera changed direction to block their path. Could their journey get any worse? What had she done to deserve this torment? If God did answer her, the thrum of her heartbeat would drown Him out.

"Do not dismount from this mule," Eliab cautioned. "Remember the Moabites. You have an advantage with height when you strike."

"I remember." She wished she could curl up and hide. Fly away to a safe place. A familiar place. And flee this wilderness of Benjamin.

Gera halted a few yards away. The men riding with him flanked his sides, forming a battle line.

Eliab grabbed the reins. "I will not leave you. I will be dead before I let Gera take my betrothed."

"Wife," she said, stretching to her full height but leaving a hand on his waist. "I'm your wife." Her breathy proclamation hung in the air. And for once, it did not scare her.

"You are." His arm pinned hers to his side in a possessive hold. "Always."

The solid warmth of his body reassured her laboring heart. At least for the moment.

A brazen grin crept up Gera's face as he watched Eliab bleed. He rode forth until his mule stood neck to neck with their mount.

"Is she too much for you, Eliab? Let me savor her bruising."

A sucking sound coming from Gera's lips caused her stomach to heave. She covered her mouth in a gesture of shock.

The accompanying men chuckled at their leader's suggestive sounds. Eliab tensed. She felt every ridge and bump under her grasp.

"Watch your mouth." Eliab spit out the rebuke with enough force to quiet the cackling. "Do you mean to bring judgment upon me as your family did upon our brothers?" Eliab scanned the men, stopping his gaze upon a younger Benjamite. "Abihu, did my father not defend your household before the council? Did he not give his word that you were not in the town square?"

Gera chastised the boy with a scowl. "And what did Berek bring upon Benjamin but destruction?"

"Because he would not hand your brothers over to the elders." Eliab's shout rang in her ears. A trickle of blood from an unbound gash on Eliab's shoulder snaked down her arm.

I beg of You, Lord, send me Your angels, for I need to get Eliab home.

Gera urged his mount forward so he sat inches from Eliab. The pungent odor of days-old sweat filled her nostrils. She leaned away from Gera's stench.

Eliab seemed to ignore his foe. He lifted his left arm and pointed at Gera's men.

"The household of Berek serves the One True God. The God of Abraham, Isaac, and Jacob. Stand with the remaining elders of our tribe. There are not enough of us left to fight each other."

Gera scoffed at Eliab. "Did your brother Ashbanel not share a bed with my sister and her idols?"

"No." The correction came from behind Gera's men.

Berek rode through the row of scoffers, parting their line and bumping Abihu's mount. The boy's mule bucked. Losing heart, Abihu trotted off with another of Gera's men. Dust kicked up by spooked hooves masked their retreat.

Eliab pulled their mule away from Gera.

Berek and Isa sat high on their mounts among Gera's scattering followers. A few men followed in Berek's wake and kept the cowards from sneaking back to the city.

Naomi crumpled against Eliab's back. She exhaled so long she could not remember the last time she had breathed in. *Thank You, Lord*. God had sent them defenders.

Parading in front of the crowd, Berek assessed every man, eye to eye, before turning around and halting in front of Gera. "I believe my oldest, Ashbanel, pleasured in your sister, but not in her gods." Berek bellowed his correction. His stare rested on Gera. "Do not make me regret protecting a few of our men, for all of us have suffered because of their transgressions."

"Can we not converse with a brother?" Gera shrugged. "I believe you have misjudged us, Elder.

Allow me to make amends and we will be on our way." Gera signaled for his men to disperse. He rode closer to Eliab's mount. She turned her head, for even looking at the devious liar churned her stomach.

Berek allowed Gera privacy for his apology.

"Forgive me." Gera's voice boomed, but it held no remorse. "But why shouldn't I delight in your pain? You've had two wives and left me with none."

"Liar." Eliab lunged at Gera.

She jerked sideways. "Eliab," she screamed, trying to right herself and keep them from falling to the ground. She yanked on his tunic and caught the edge of a bloody bandage that came loose in her hand.

Eliab winced.

Served him right for acting like a fool. She knew Gera to be vile, but his claim about Eliab having another betrothed made her want to slap someone. She withdrew her hands from Eliab's waist.

Backing his mule over a few feet of parched soil, Gera regarded her form with uninvited interest. "Your Ephraimite whore should take better care of you, Eliab."

She fisted Eliab's bandage and hurled it at Gera with a slinger's aim. Bloodstained cloth slid down his nasty face with its gaping mouth.

"Filthy hog. Go wash yourself," she shouted.

Isa and Berek hurried toward Eliab.

Retreating with what were left of his men, Gera kept his unclean face averted.

Berek's expression soured as he scanned his son's injuries. "What did that coward do to you?"

"I chased a goat off a cliff. If Naomi had not been with me, I would still be sleeping on the side of a mountain." Eliab relaxed against her chest.

Isa tilted Eliab's chin and observed his eyes. "I worried when you did not arrive with my livestock. Do you see more than one of me?"

"One is enough." Eliab tried to smile, but grunted instead as he shifted his weight. "I'm glad you are in need of me. Though next time, I will herd the sheep."

"The ewe?" Isa asked.

A lump grew in Naomi's throat as she recalled the mother's desperate eyes. "My hands were full. I could not carry another."

Berek untethered her mule. The animal did not seem unnerved by the commotion. "We must get my son home and care for his wounds."

"Naomi can tend to my needs." Eliab kicked at his mule's sides and guided it in the direction of East Gibeah.

She would tend to Eliab because her fate was aligned with his, but her temples throbbed as tendrils of envy wrapped around her insides. Eliab had never mentioned another woman. She leaned in close to his ear. "I hope my talents measure up to your previous wife's."

14

Berek settled Eliab onto a mat in the corner of the living area. Naomi grabbed a jar in order to fill a basin with water. So lightweight was the empty vessel that it practically lifted itself. But why was it empty? Hadn't Cuzbi filled the pots while she was risking her life on the hilly trails? If only she could smash the pottery without a reprimand. Nothing like being threatened by Gera and lied to by her supposed husband. Her family could not arrive fast enough. The sooner her tribe came, the better. What was taking them so long?

She stomped into the cooking courtyard, ready to charge at anything or anyone. Someone grasped her shoulder. Her chest heaved. She whipped around, ready to fight.

"Cuzbi," she rasped, "I thought you were Gera."

"Gera? That boar of a man who chastised my husband? Oh, Naomi." Cuzbi pulled her into an embrace. "I heard of Eliab's fall. Will he heal? Can he still father a child?"

Naomi ripped free from Cuzbi. This was not a customary apology or consolation. Curses hung on her lips, but she swallowed them. "What is wrong with you? Have you been drinking again?"

Cuzbi stepped backward. "No." She stretched out her response like a disobedient child. "I learned my lesson last night. And this morning." She rubbed her temple. "According to my husband, I spoke forthright from the spirits."

Cuzbi's casual use of *husband* fueled Naomi's ire. Her friend had most readily accepted being kidnapped. Naomi rubbed her hand on her robe. Where would she be this morning if Eliab had not shown restraint and honored her request for time? She shuddered at the thought of a stranger stroking her skin—a thought Cuzbi seemed to have embraced without consideration of her family's honor.

Remembering her task, Naomi rushed to get clean water. "I cannot tarry. Eliab needs my attention."

Cuzbi scurried after her. "You have decided to stay then?"

Naomi filled her jar from the containers in the courtyard. She pointed at Cuzbi. "I need some oil, hyssop, and herbs."

As she passed by her friend, Cuzbi took hold with such strength that Naomi nearly drenched their clothes.

"I need you, Naomi. Look around us. Did you not want to marry a landowner? We have fields and you know how to till them. Who will loom the garments for me to barter? You weave for the best merchants." A tear strayed from Cuzbi's lashes. "Stay and raise children with me. Be my midwife and I will be yours."

Berek's summons for assistance bellowed from inside the dwelling.

She clutched her vessel tighter so as not to waste a single drop.

"Open your eyes." Cuzbi's grip was a tourniquet upon Naomi's arm. "Stay."

Friendship, duty, and despair bore down on Naomi like sacks of grain on a mule's withers. Her lips parted but she did not know what to say. Should she stay to be near her friend or to be wed to a landowner? Didn't she deserve more from a marriage? Didn't her family deserve consideration? Her thoughts blurred. Since the festival, hardly anything made sense.

"I need the oil and herbs. Please hurry." She backed away from Cuzbi and stomped into the house.

Eliab, half-awake, tried to smile at her as she dropped by his side and dampened a cloth. Removing the blood from his face would be her first task. He winced as she swiped his cheek.

"Are you planning on leaving any skin?"

She lightened her touch and wrung out the rag.

Eliab glanced at where his father and brother sat huddled at the table in fervent discussion.

"If you are upset at Gera's words, you needn't be. He misspoke," Eliab muttered. "I had a short betrothal, but no wife."

"Then what Gera said had some truth in it. You lied to me." Heat rushed through her body. She began to rise. "Scrub your own chin."

Eliab grabbed her arm.

"Don't leave. Stay and I will tell you everything." His voice was strained.

She hesitated. Ripping her arm from his grasp would hurt Eliab. She didn't wish that. She cared. A little. And she had a lot of curiosity. Had Eliab spent much time in this girl's household? And if he had, could he forget his feelings for her? Is that why he'd waited in the grove? She wanted to know—had to know—in order to banish the accusations from her mind.

"I will listen. There are not many places where I can go." When he released her arm, she sat back down, making sure their bodies did not touch.

Eliab rested his back against the wall. "My father arranged for me to marry a Reubenite. I visited her home near Jericho twice. Once to meet her family and share a meal. Another time to sit with her and her mother and a few aunts to talk. The war began shortly after my second journey."

She twisted a rag in the basin. "You were not alone with her?"

"I did not kiss her." The words rushed from his mouth. "I have only kissed one woman other than my mother and my sisters." He stroked her knee with a feather-like caress from his battered arm.

The pulsating beat of her heart deafened her ears. She glanced to see if Ashbanel and Berek took notice. They continued their whispered debate.

"Ours was a celebratory kiss, I am told, but go on." She used his closeness to wipe his neck.

His gaze locked on hers. His eyes danced with little lights like dust falling from the stars. She looked away and concentrated on her task. It must have been the lamp.

"It meant more to me," he said. "I want to kiss you again, and not just a celebratory kiss. I want to kiss you as a husband who knows the tender places upon his wife's body."

She licked her lips. Thinking about kissing Eliab jumbled her nerves. She would not be hearing such requests if her father sat nearby, overseeing their meeting. She dipped her hands in the bowl, but her mouth felt as dry as shed snakeskin.

"You don't know that, Eliab. You don't know me."

"I do know you. I knew you when you ran to help Jael. When you agreed to dance to save our lives. And when you saved me from my fall. To me you are a sunrise. A way out of the darkness. I never felt this way with the other girl."

Reminded of their original topic, she stiffened and removed his hand from her knee.

"I asked you to recall what you did with her. If you were left by yourselves."

His hand stayed where she had placed it.

"We spoke of our families mostly. Her mother and aunts were part of the conversation. Her father owned livestock, and we would stroll to look at the animals. During my second visit, the Levite and his wife came to stay in Gibeah. That is when Gera's kin whipped the crowd into a frenzy and they tried to coax the Levite to come and join in their orgy. The Levite must live with his decision to send his wife into the night to suffer abuse. When my intended's father learned of the grievances against my tribe, he took the vow and broke our betrothal."

"No wives for Benjamites." Her chest ached when she tallied another woman that Eliab had lost in the conflict. She dabbed at some dried blood on his leg. Her hand was too unsteady to bathe the rest of his face.

"So you see, I never had a wife. I never rode with her or lay beside her. I've never had a marriage union." His brown eyes begged for understanding.

What did he want her to say? That she was wrong to be upset? Did he want an apology? Did he want her to admit she was jealous? Was she?

"Thank you for your honesty." Her words came out weak and breathy and not with the bold sincerity she would have liked. "I do not know about your past, and I cannot learn if there are secrets kept from me. We have an agreement, so I should know things about you as an intended."

"We do have an agreement, and I will honor it." He grimaced as he repositioned his body. "I was an angry man when I hid in the grove. God had seen fit to punish my people, take my family, and my betrothed. I did not want to grab a stranger from a feast. But then you came to me. Right into my arms." He smiled at the remembrance and leaned closer, brushing a strand of hair from her face. "I want you to want to stay in East Gibeah. Together, we can ease our grief."

A bead of sweat trickled from her temple to her throat. Try as she might to rinse her washcloth, she fumbled the rag, splashing the floor.

Eliab picked up the cloth and held it. "Gera accuses me of having two wives, but I have never known a woman. I cannot say the same for him." He cleared his throat and glanced across the room. "That blasphemer partook in several orgies to please the idols. I preferred to follow God's ways. I still do." He reached out and handed her the rag. "That is my truth."

The intensity of his expression said he wanted to be her husband. Her cheeks burned hot with understanding while her heart drummed a rhythm in her ribs, in her belly, and inches below. These feelings were not supposed to happen so soon. Months, even years, passed from the time of the annual festival to a betrothal period to a marriage bed. Not days.

"I need to get fresh water." And some air. And a clear head.

She dashed outside and almost ran into Isa. Gasping, she covered her mouth and gaped at him cradling a large wooly bundle. He held her injured ewe.

Flinging the water into the dirt, she dropped the

basin and brushed the mother's coat with her fingertips.

"You brought her. Oh, Isa. You rescued my gift." Tears welled in her eyes. "How can I ever repay this debt?"

"Debt?" Isa's eyes widened. He swayed as if in shock. "You stayed behind to comfort Jael. If you had not detained Eliab, I would be dead, and I cannot think upon what those pagans would have done to my girl." Isa shook his head and shuddered.

Jael? Naomi had forgotten about her young friend. She was not in the courtyard with Cuzbi.

"Where is Jael?" She kept her voice low so as not to frighten the ewe.

Isa grinned. "If I know her, she is asleep in the sheep's pen with a big stick nearby. We will tend to this one while you tend to Eliab."

"Toda raba." The words harbored in her throat. "You have made my heart sing." She kissed the sheep's head.

Isa started to leave. He stopped a few steps away.

"I hope you stay in East Gibeah, even if Ephraim should come."

His words squeezed her soul. "Why do you say this?" Was there a conspiracy this night to convince her to remain in Benjamin?

Isa readjusted his hold on her ewe. "Today I glimpsed the Eliab I knew in the fields. The only thing that has changed since the war is that you are here. I can never repay Eliab for burying my family." Isa raised up her gift. "This is a start. *Shalom.*" With a nod, he turned and traipsed into the darkening landscape.

Naomi listened to Isa's footfalls fade away. Perhaps God wanted her to stay in East Gibeah after all. This morning, she would have run into her father's arms and left Benjamin behind, but now a small part of her wished to stay. Was it solely sympathy keeping her with this struggling tribe? Sympathy for Cuzbi, Jael, and Isa? Or was a fondness for the brave and wounded Eliab taking root in her heart?

Turning, she found Eliab standing in the doorway.

"Your gift has returned."

A tear trickled down her cheek. She swiped it away. "You need to go lie down. I am not finished with you yet."

"Those are the best words I've heard all day, for you are my gift."

Her countenance caved like a stone tumbling from its tower. *Oh, Eliab.* Did he know what he was asking of her?

15

Naomi rested against the smooth-stone doorway to Eliab's room. One leg dangled over the ledge of the upper room, swinging and slicing the warm night air. The ladder sat sideways near where Eliab slept. She spied no rows of vines in the distance, no clusters of olive trees, only barren rock and spoiled ground. Where were her father, her brother, her tribe? Nothing moved in the dark. Had she been transported to a new city her family did not know of? Was this God's answer to her prayer? That she should stay?

A shuffling sound caught her attention. Eliab struggled to rise from his bed. With his injuries, he had not positioned a hand upon her hip to wake him if she moved.

"It is too far to jump." He grunted as he limped closer.

"After your fall, I would surely use the ladder."

He did not sit on the opposite side of the threshold. Instead, he settled behind her with the wall as his backrest and his legs stretched in front. The rush of his breath sounded like a storm wind. If she fell back, she would lie in his lap with nowhere to look but his rugged face.

"You should rest," she said. Oh, why did she care?

"Whether I sleep or stand, my bones cry out. Perhaps they woke you?" A bit of humor echoed in his voice.

Even in the dark, she could feel his gaze upon the side of her face. He liked to be close. Too close. But she needed distance from him, from Gibeah, from the stirrings he created deep inside of her.

"I am accustomed to the groans of pain." She did not like how harsh her words made her seem.

"As we all are." He peeked from the doorway, his cheek brushing hers. "My father has placed scouts in the hills. They will warn us if the men of Ephraim come."

"If? My family will come. My father will fight to restore his honor and to seek restitution for the payment he has lost." She faced him, knowing his eyes and lips would be temptingly close. "You had sisters. You spoke enough that I know you would pursue their captors."

"I would have." He choked on his reply as if speaking of his sisters caused him more pain than his injuries.

She dropped her gaze into her lap. Regret weighed upon her conscience, for she was not the only one who suffered loss. "Forgive me. I should not have brought them up."

He reached out and stroked her hair, but her curls would not stay tucked behind her ear. Her mother had tried over and over to brush her ringlets into submission. She would not reveal how the tug on her scalp, the tenderness of his caress, took her to another place—a safe and happier place.

"It does not bother me." His fingers brushed strands from her cheekbone and she withheld a shudder. "When you speak of them, it does not feel as though they are really gone. And you are right—I would have pursued their captors to the depths of the sea. But we did not lie in wait in Shiloh for revenge or as part of a wicked scheme."

"You stole our daughters." She untangled his hand from her hair and resettled it on his leg.

"Only at the urging of some elders."

"Whose elders?" Her heart pounded as if she had run to the well and back.

"Some elders of Judah. One had married a woman from Shiloh. He knew of the harvest festival and suggested we take wives in the night to uphold the oath."

She tucked her legs beneath her, ready to hear more of this news. "You speak as if Ephraim should turn a blind eye to this plan. I doubt in my heart if the elders of Ephraim would have allowed this plot."

"Yet they have not come to Gibeah."

His explanation hummed in her ears. Was her decision already made for her? Was Ephraim not coming to her rescue? Had the council leaders found a way around the oath? Her pulse pounded the questions through her brain.

As if sensing her confusion, Eliab held her face gently. His face was the only form she could make out in the shadows.

"I care for you, Naomi. Our betrothal is not like others, but I want to be your husband. Can you learn to make this your home?"

Taking his hands, she wrapped them in hers and held them to her rib cage. She cast a glance out into the darkness. What if her brother Nadab waited there? If he came forward now, would she leave with him? The scent of hyssop filled the threshold. Had she not saved Eliab and bathed his wounds like a wife? Eliab wanted an answer. An answer she could not give without betraying her family and her tribe. He caressed her hand, his finger tracing a path around her palm. Each small circle frayed her composure.

"I am tired." Her raspy tone told the truth. "Is it not enough for you that I am here now? We are betrothed until the Sabbath. I made a vow before God which I cannot break."

Eliab struggled to rise. "Come to bed with me. We both need rest and—"

"And?" She licked her lips and remained perched in the doorway.

"Comfort." He stepped toward the mat. "I made the vow before God too. I will honor our covenant." The hurt that rumbled in his words did not seem to come from his gashes.

Following in his wake, she lay beside him, careful not to bump his wounds. He positioned himself on his side like he did the first night. She brought a clean sheet up over their bodies.

"Eliab," she whispered. "Why did you agree to wait?"

Silence.

Was he already asleep?

"You were scared," he said in a wisp of a voice. "And I was angry."

"Are you still?" She swallowed hard. "Angry, I mean. Or confused?"

"Not anymore." His hand rested on her hip, the familiar weight bearing down on her bone. "Are you still afraid of me?"

"Not now." Her reply slipped out easily, as if she'd refused wine with dinner.

"Then sleep."

She tried to rest but stared wide-eyed into the

dark. Her conversation with Eliab raced through her mind. She cared for him. Fighting it was useless. But then maybe she would feel differently in the light of day with people around and work to finish. They were too close in his bedroom, too intimate in their talk. Closing her eyes, she thought of nothing, concentrating on the shadows and shapes behind her eyelids.

When sunlight brightened the upper room, she woke alone and hurried to find Eliab. He was outside, and he boasted that her *gift* had lambed during the night.

"Did you not think to come and get me when Isa brought news of the birth?" She hoped her ewe fared well after such a long journey the previous day. Finally, some joy had come to her in this odd land.

"You had fallen asleep. Besides, you did not need to wash my wounds in the early hours of the morning."

Of course she needed to. She was his betrothed, and he had cried out in his slumber, but she did not want to argue. Her skin pimpled at the thought of holding her newborn lamb. If her ewe ailed, she would stay at Isa's and see to her comfort.

Naomi tugged Eliab toward Isa's thatched-roof house. She slowed her pace when Eliab fell behind, hurrying him along with a wave of her hand.

"You are certain the mother fared well?" she asked.

Eliab clapped a hand upon her shoulder. "Isa and I have birthed livestock for years in Gibeah."

"But never mine." She bit her lip as they neared Isa's modest home.

Isa waved to them from a fenced area.

Eliab limped a little faster.

Naomi rushed to peek into the sheep's pen. She had chided Eliab to let her keep the mother as a gift, something of her own in this foreign place, but now she had a gift to give him—the start to a herd. She rubbed a hand over the worn wood and wondered if she would be here to see a full herd.

She peeked over the fencing. "He's black?" The shock in her voice brought the lamb teetering her direction. The mother bleated from her straw bed, chastising her offspring. "There was no dark ram in the ravine."

Isa crossed the pen with Jael on his heels. "Not that we saw. And on him I can find no blemish."

"He's perfect," Jael said. "And I helped bring him forth."

Isa stood in front of the gate, but he did not open it.

"She has smaller hands." The boy beamed as he praised Jael's feat.

Jael cuddled the lamb in her arms.

Eliab struggled to bend and inspect the newborn. He glanced toward Isa, who shooed off a wayward yearling. Balancing his weight on the edge of the fence, Eliab patted the young sheep.

Naomi reached in to touch her lamb. Her fingers tangled with Eliab's as the lamb wiggled in Jael's arms. She did not pull away. Perhaps she should have in public, but touching Eliab had become familiar, and if she were to admit it, she had grown accustomed to his caress.

The newborn licked Eliab's face with fervor. Even though his skin was the color of a plum, he allowed the lamb to show its affection, lick after lick. Eliab covered the lamb's mouth with his hand, but the young one's tongue still threaded between his fingers. "Two gifts in one."

"Yes. A gift for both of us." For her shepherd. She placed a hand to her mouth, thankful she had not spoken aloud. Her elation at the lamb's birth seemed to have carried over into her thoughts.

"Yom, stop that." Jael pulled the lamb away from Eliab. "He is full of spirit."

"You named him?" Her heart stuttered. Shouldn't Jael have consulted her before naming the lamb? If only Eliab had awakened her sooner.

Isa swung his arm toward a few yearlings wandering near the fence. "He is the color of night, but we call him Day, for today is a new beginning for our herdsmen. Perhaps it is a new day for all of us. We will have flocks in Benjamin, but ours will be like no other."

Jael laughed as Yom nibbled her collar. "And I will help birth them all."

Naomi's cheeks warmed. She bit her lip while Jael took the lamb over to *her* gift to suckle. Couldn't she be the one to see to the ewe's needs? Isa guarded the gate as if she was his enemy and he was the only shepherd in East Gibeah.

Naomi placed a hand on the gate. "We shall watch over the herd and give you rest."

Isa shrugged. "There is no need. We are taking turns." Isa shifted closer to Eliab. "Jael is content when she assists me, especially with the lamb." He gave Eliab a nudge.

"We will return when I am stronger," Eliab said.

Isa stifled a yawn. "And then we will go in search of more blessings."

Eliab clapped Isa on the back and winced at the pain of raising his arm. "*Toda raba.*" He rested a more delicate hand on her. "Let us go."

She shook her head. A stinging pressure built behind her eyes. "I didn't get to hold the newborn." Her whispered words caught in her windpipe.

Eliab's head blocked her view of the pen. "They are working well together. We do not want to intrude."

Look around you, Naomi. Hadn't Cuzbi warned her to fit in here? Become a Benjamite? Jael was all giggles and laughter with Isa and his sheep. *God, I feel so alone.* Her face burned, but not from the sun. Was she ready to tell Eliab she saw a hint of a future, here, with him? Her breaths came too fast. She had to get away from the pen. Crying would draw attention to her distress and she did not want Jael to be upset.

She hurried down the path.

Eliab followed. He did not call her name until they were a good distance from Isa's house.

She ignored his summons. She didn't want to explain her feelings. She was acting foolish and she knew it, but didn't she have a right to be hurt?

Gasps of pain accompanied Eliab's plea to wait.

If his wounds opened, infection could set in. She stopped and paced back and forth. She swore a spinning wheel whirled in her chest.

With a hand to her waist, Eliab stilled her movements.

"There is a cave nearby. We held sheep in it when we needed cover from the sun or a rest." He dipped his head, but she did not meet his gaze. He would want to talk. He would want an answer for her behavior.

How could she tell him of her sins? I am selfish with my lamb. Jealous of Jael. Filled with guilt about my family. Was Cuzbi correct? Should she have buried herself beneath Eliab's blanket that first night?

Forgotten she was the daughter of Heriah? How could she spend the night next to him and admit to feelings of lust?

"If you lead the way, I will follow." Her tone was as flat as the field they stood in.

Eliab huffed as he descended two steps into the sunken cavern. A few boulders lodged outside a cave. Naomi looked up several feet to the ground on which they had walked just a few moments before. She sat on a rounded rock and Eliab nestled next to her. His fingers caressed the back of her hand. He said nothing. He asked nothing. He just was.

His patience loosened a confession from her lips.

"I should have been the one to name the lamb. The ewe is my gift. A gift from my betrothed."

She waited for a response. None came.

Taking a deep breath, she continued, "I do not have anything in East Gibeah. No family. Few friends. No friends without husbands," she added quickly. "No loom. I don't even have my indigo sash." She willed herself not to cry. She spoke the truth. Her truth. "Everything has changed too fast."

Eliab's hand stilled. He lifted her chin until she could not help but look into his eyes, her reflection filling the brown-and-amber rings. "You have me." His fingers stroked her face and felt as soft as silk. She shivered at his caress. "If you want me?"

Her heartbeat thrummed everywhere but in her chest as his breath breezed over her cheek. His expression was that of a caged lion. Caged for the moment.

She licked her lips, but they dried beneath his breathing. Did he want another celebratory kiss? Or did he want more? A blossom opened within her belly.

She liked Eliab's closeness. She liked Eliab's stolen kiss. Try as she may to fight it, she liked Eliab.

Eliab shifted closer.

Would he act if she did not?

Her body floated above the boulder like a dragonfly. She brushed his cheek with the kiss of a gracious host and then pulled away.

"I believe a swarm of gnats breezed by my face."

He sat there, silent, unmoving.

She glanced at where his hand still rested upon her fist. "I am not accustomed to your manner of kissing."

"As it should be. You have not had a wedding night." His words rasped with a yearning. "I will be a good husband. I will try to give you what you want."

She fought the emotions flooding her soul. "I know you will."

"I believe part of you likes it here, with me."

"It does." Her admission did not seem so difficult. A brief smile bubbled to her lips.

Eliab slid a finger over the curve of her mouth and bent low, placing a kiss upon her parted lips.

All the barriers she had placed and misplaced fell away. She pressed her mouth against his, inviting him to linger.

"Naomi!"

She jumped. Of all the times to be interrupted.

Eliab pulled away.

Cuzbi charged forward into the stone shepherd's pen. "There you are. Must I find you when work is to be done? Come to the well with me."

"I filled the jars this morning." Couldn't this chore wait? She tried not to flinch as Eliab slid a hand down her back. She would have sworn her lips had plumped, giving her breach of discretion away.

Cuzbi crinkled her nose at them. Had she seen their kiss?

"What is of importance in this pit?"

"I am comforting Naomi." Eliab's tone was more of chastisement than explanation.

"Well, I need her now." Cuzbi punched her hands into her hips. "Fire overtook the cooking courtyard."

"The entire area?" Naomi glanced at Eliab. He indicated she should go with her friend. Standing and leaving the warmth of Eliab's body sent a shiver cascading over her skin.

She held onto Cuzbi's arm and hurried toward the courtyard.

If only Cuzbi knew how close Naomi was to deciding to stay. Then maybe Cuzbi wouldn't have almost burned their house down.

16

Cuzbi cackled as they marched toward the house of Berek. She seemed too gleeful for having set their courtyard aflame.

"How did the fire start?" Naomi asked.

"Some kindling ignited and burned your herbs, but I do not believe the flames were as large as the ones blazing in that sunken cave."

Naomi's eyes widened. "Surely you do not think?"

"Do not be ashamed." Cuzbi stifled another giggle. "You heeded my words and seduced him. I must confess I was worried that after his fall he would not be a fitting husband. Crushed by rocks and everything." Cuzbi veered in the direction of the cooking courtyard and let her wanton words trail off. "I am glad you are making an effort. A little boldness becomes you."

Pressing her lips together, Naomi held her reply. The only boldness she showed with Eliab was asking for a betrothal. And now after all the hours she had spent with him, she almost wished she had not made a vow to keep herself from him.

"Eliab and I are getting to know one another. In our own time."

"So I see."

Rubbing her temples, Naomi sought to end

Cuzbi's banter. "I do not need advice. My mother spoke outright when I went into the vineyards."

"Oh, come now. You need some encouragement." Cuzbi laughed as she flung open the gate. "I had to practically pull you into the procession of dancers at the festival."

"I would have shown myself to the crowd in good time."

"In good time may not have been the right time. You needed me to coax you to the front."

"And look what we reaped. We were the first ones plucked by the Benjamites." Naomi bent to pick up a jar. She stood and positioned a jug on her shoulder. "I am learning to live in this land, but I cannot help but struggle with the manner in which these men sought us out. My father was not shown any respect. What time was my mother given to arrange her household without a daughter to assist her?"

Cuzbi seized a vessel lying near the fire pit. "Your husband is the son of an elder, and from what I saw in that pit, you are encouraging his affections."

"What other choice have I been given?"

"None. But Eliab is your best choice. Throw your lot in with him and stop thinking too much."

Without thinking too much at all, Naomi knew she liked Eliab's strength, faith, and character.

Swinging her jar, Cuzbi quick-stepped past the ashen remains of dried plants. "I bartered beside my father in the market for two years. I said it was this price, and it was so. Did the landowner not say to you, 'Pick this row' or 'Till this soil'? My father told you what to weave and it came forth."

Cuzbi drew to her full height as Naomi darted through the courtyard gate ahead of Cuzbi.

"Accept your fate as I have and stop waiting for another to tell you of your blessings."

Naomi whirled around. "And what of my brothers who died upon these rocks? I worked to make up their wages. If Ephraim shall come to claim us, what does my father reap?" Reliving the weight of her brothers' loss, Naomi's chest heaved. Her throat needed a drink from these empty vessels. "Nothing is growing here. Will our fathers leave empty-handed?"

Cuzbi clicked her tongue and shook her head. "Your old way of life is behind you now. Ashbanel and Berek will one day have riches. Will they not make sure Eliab has flocks to tend? My words were meant in praise of your actions, not to anger you."

Anger? No, try guilt. Naomi's mouth gaped, but she had no response for her friend. Lush fields did not grow in Gibeah. Merchants did not clamor for her woven wares. But Eliab lived in this land, and try as she might to fight her feelings, she cared about him, but she also cared about the well-being of her family.

Before she could assemble an apology for her outburst, Berek emerged from the stable. Naomi secured her jar and gave a reverent knee bob. Cuzbi bowed. Had Berek heard their conversation? Her heartbeat galloped like a wild horse, for she had not sung Benjamin's praises like her friend.

"My daughters." Berek acknowledged their respect and enfolded them into his family without a blink. "Where is my son Eliab?" He shielded his eyes and searched the horizon.

"He is overseeing the sheep in Isa's care," Naomi said. "I must assist in carrying water from the well."

"Hmm, yes." Berek answered as if he wished to forget Cuzbi's mishap. "Take my mule and fill the skins as well."

The elder disappeared into the stable and returned with his gray mule. Balancing her jug, Naomi received the reins from Berek.

"Go in peace," he said before returning to his task.

"I will ride." Cuzbi set her jar on the ground and mounted the mule before Naomi could stop her ascent.

Naomi tensed. "Berek gave me the lead."

Cuzbi leaned forward, inches from Naomi's face. "I was the first one taken."

"Do you refer to the festival or the trail?" She shoved a jar into Cuzbi's chest.

Cuzbi scoffed and looked away.

Naomi urged the mule forward. Her clay vessel blocked her view of her friend.

"I may be with child."

She let the trade winds blow Cuzbi's announcement into the hills. The same loneliness that had crept into her soul while Jael harbored the lamb gripped her anew, but she could not stay silent. "So soon?"

"I judge it to be true, and in a few days' time I will be certain."

Lowering her jug, Naomi smiled at Cuzbi and at the thought of a baby. "Now you truly are a Benjamite." She struggled to bring glee to her tone.

Cuzbi twisted the reins into a thick rope. "I am pleased to have a family of my own. You do not know what it is like to be cast off. Men do not look upon me the same way they look upon you, Naomi. You are blind if you do not see it."

"That is untrue." She met Cuzbi's heavy-lidded gaze. "I grew up with brothers; you had only sisters. That is the difference. Besides, you spoke with men every day in the markets, something I could not do."

"To do business, yes. They did not want more from me. Why do you think I danced for so many years at the feast?"

"You bargained well for your father." That was truth. Her family spoke of Cuzbi's shrewdness. "Your father may have seemed like he would not honor a betrothal."

"That is because no offers came." Cuzbi shook her head. "Men looked at me, but their eyes did not linger. With you dancing beside me, I thought I could catch someone's interest. And I did. Do not judge me too harshly. I am content here. I feel wanted for the first time in my life."

"I know in my heart there is a clamoring for your return. Your father was overjoyed with the extra shekels you brought him. Customers returned because you remembered their tastes and sold the best wares. Seeing your skill prompted me to weave better robes."

"I will never go back." Cuzbi's face grew somber. "Someone else can work our booth. My sisters can learn to trade, for there is no passion in my blood for bartering. I have a husband now."

Taking hold of Cuzbi's arm, Naomi rested her head upon her friend's shoulder for an instant, just enough of an embrace to clear the harsh words spoken on their journey. "Forgive me for not seeing your unhappiness. I will not judge you, if you do not judge me. For with all the burdens I carry with me from Shiloh, I am warming to a Benjamite's touch. Woe to anyone who does not consider our plight."

"Oh, sister, you have always made me believe I have something of value to offer others."

"Just not your cooking."

All the way to the well, Cuzbi laughed and Naomi joined in.

Casting off the stone and filling skins unwound Naomi's muscles. What was such light labor to a grape picker's daughter?

Cuzbi rode on the return trip. "I may need some help scrubbing walls when we return."

Naomi suppressed a smile. "Shall I keep you from strong arms with which to hold your son?"

"Yes, and you'd better be ready to deliver my heir when he arrives."

As they neared the courtyard, Eliab waved his good arm while occupying the doorway to his upper room. At least his right arm was raised, even if it didn't sway.

"Come and be swift." The fervor in his voice rose toward the sky.

The glances from her friend had Naomi's cheeks simmering. Couldn't Eliab see she had a task at hand? Besides, what was new in his bedroom?

She took Cuzbi's jar and helped her dismount. Eliab could wait. Did he think her a servant too? Being hospitable to a friend was customary, and he should understand her delay.

He beckoned her again.

Was his room on fire?

Leaving the vessels at the courtyard wall, she climbed the steps to Eliab's room. Why was everyone in such a hurry this day?

Eliab stepped to the side of the threshold. Good. Or she would ram him like a cedar rod.

"What do you think?" His eyebrows rose as he gestured toward the back of the room.

Did he expect a bedding after one kiss? Of all the

foolish schemes—

She gasped and hurried toward a loom with a wooden frame and threaded like a harp, waiting for a weaver.

Warmth drained from her face. Her flesh pimpled like a naked slave readied for bidding.

"You are a woman of your word." Eliab's feet shuffled across the floor until she felt his presence at her side. "You've promised Jael a garment. And now you have a loom."

"Where did you get these planks and the thread?" She stepped forward and ran her fingers over the taut strings. She stroked the wool as if it were silk.

"My father and Jael went into Gibeah when we were in the hills. They found enough wood, and a merchant graciously showed my father where women had hidden supplies before the battles. This is what you had in Shiloh. Jael was sure of it." His hands clasped behind his hips like a child waiting for praise. "You desired to weave, did you not?"

"Yes, yes, I did." Her chest ached to bursting.

His expression grew jubilant.

She left the loom and slipped her arms under his cloak. The aroma of hyssop and lamb's wool filled her senses. She held him, not too tight as to cause him pain, but close enough that she could feel the warmth from his tunic. His hand settled on her waist.

She gazed into those eyes that made her body a tree about to bud. "I suppose you would like another kiss?"

"You are the guest, and I am the host." His voice rumbled from deep within his chest. "Take what you would like."

"No," she whispered. "I am not the guest. Where

the host lives is my home as well." She took his face in her hands and pressed her lips into his, promising a celebration that would soon come to pass as long as forgiveness lived in the hearts of her tribesmen.

17

Naomi finished another row of weave and tapped it taut with her comb. If one could find peace from laboring, she found it in her loom, a skill from Shiloh taking root in Benjamin. She welcomed the tingle of strands on her fingertips. For a moment, she had found refuge from thoughts of war and revenge.

Behind her, the rhythm of fingers splitting bean pods halted.

"You have worked steadily since last eve. It is almost time for prayer." Jael swiped her hands together and sent dust wafting into the air.

"This is not a burden." Naomi threaded her paddle to begin another run. "I promised you a new tunic and now I have the means to provide it."

"So you are content to stay here as Eliab's wife?" A hint of curiosity rang in Jael's question, but Naomi heard undertones of hesitation.

Securing her pattern, Naomi knelt beside Jael. "Do you desire to return to Shiloh?"

"No!"

Naomi's mouth gaped at her friend's outburst.

"I have a future here with Isa. When we come together, I hope to have many children, but we are waiting, not unlike others, until we know no harm will come to him. He does not want me and his child to be a burden to my mother. And in time, we will fill the hillside with livestock. My mother can join us when she is able. I will finally have a way to take care of her." Jael gathered the basket of beans to her chest. "I was uncertain of you."

"Of me?" Naomi stood and smoothed her robe. Where did she begin to explain how her initial hatred toward the tribe that had killed her brothers and the guilt from a betrothal to a Benjamite had turned into love? Love? She had not even said that word to Eliab. She could barely admit it to herself.

Jael stared and waited. She made no effort to fill the silence.

"It is true I believed all Benjamites to be wicked. And why not? They rebelled against our laws. Killed our people. At times, I wanted revenge for the blood of my brothers. I cannot think of their loss without sorrow, but now I have seen how people have suffered here in Gibeah."

"Do you still seek a punishment?" Jael's brow furrowed.

Naomi plopped onto the floor and snapped open a bean pod. "I would be a liar if I said I have forgiven the blaspheming Benjamites. But in Eliab I have found someone who follows God's laws. He has suffered alongside the lawless. I did not want to care for him—"

"Now you do?" Jael swept a husk from her lap.

Shaking her head, Naomi smiled at the thought of being wed to a man who was once her enemy. "I cannot imagine another as my husband."

"Nor I." Jael's cheeks flushed. "With Isa, I mean."

Naomi heard her name called from outside near the courtyard. It was Eliab's voice, an urgent summons. Would she grow accustomed to his demands? Tomorrow the Sabbath began at sundown.

And after one full day of rest, their vow would be fulfilled. Her stomach flipped like a newly caught fish at the thought of truly being Eliab's wife.

She scrambled to her feet and rushed down the steps with Jael at her heels. Eliab and Isa approached the house, their mounts at a charge.

Eliab struggled to dismount from his mule before it came to a halt. She had never seen his face so ruddy, not even after his fall.

He took hold of her arm. "You must come at once. We have caught a spy in the hills above Gibeah."

Lord, please do not let it be Nadab. Not her only brother. Should her father lose all his children to the Benjamites? A shiver shook her body. "Why must I see him?"

Eliab released his grip on her tunic. "Girls from the feast said you would know him."

"Is there only one?" She cleared her throat and tried to shake the warble from her words.

"Only one that we ambushed." Isa leaned forward on his mount. "There had to be others."

"Then I will see him," she said, casting a glance to Jael, then to Isa, and finally to Eliab. "I do not want any more bloodshed. You all have become like my family, and I will not lose one more to death."

Naomi followed Eliab through the streets of Gibeah to a large house. It had been rebuilt with charred rocks, but its foundation whispered of the horrors that had happened when the city lay in ruins.

She had prayed for the fighting men of Ephraim to come and rescue her, but now the petition haunted her. Surely she could not sway God's plans. A few words spoken in haste before she knew Eliab's heart would not change the will of Israel's God. At least, she hoped as much.

An inner room held the scout. No windows gave light, but an oil lamp flickered in the corner. The spy's hands were bound with rope and tied to stakes on either side of his body. He knelt with his head hung in defeat.

As if sensing he was on display, the man's head snapped upward. He glared toward the doorway with a hate that had once mirrored her own. She dodged behind the stone wall and covered her mouth to keep from crying out.

"Do you know him?" Eliab and Ashbanel chorused.

"His name is Puah. He was known by my eldest brother." Her chest tightened. Puah had mourned with her family. Mourned with her. "Why is his mouth bloody?" She cast a glance at both Eliab and Ashbanel, but her stare rested on Ashbanel.

"He struggled when we bound him." Ashbanel glanced at his prisoner with a sense of pride.

"Were there others?" Other sons of Ephraim? Her brother Nadab? Her kin?

"None that were caught." Eliab shuffled closer. "We need to gain his trust and find out if Ephraim plans to start another war."

"And you need me to petition him."

"Do us some good." The spit from Ashbanel's lips flew as fast as his demand.

"If he has been silent, who am I to get him to speak?" She bit her fingernail to gain a moment of clear thought. "He has worked with my father and brothers. I am but a girl to him. He will not inform me of battle secrets."

"Please. Try," Eliab said. "If Ephraim strikes

tonight, we have no defense. We have not even hidden the women for safety."

O God, my God. Why do You place me in such hardship?

Before she could answer, Ashbanel seized her sleeve.

She clawed at his hold, but his fat fingers held her fast.

"Go or I will tie you beside the prisoner."

"You will have to tie me first." Eliab grabbed his brother's wrist and thrust him against the wall.

She stumbled backward into the doorway. Hidden no more, she met Puah's slits for eyes. Her heart hammered against her chest.

"Heriah's daughter?"

Called upon, she stepped into the room, keeping a safe distance lest Puah free himself and attack. Eliab followed but stationed himself nearer the doorway.

"I am Naomi, Nadab's sister."

Puah wrenched his head toward Eliab. "Who is that?" The disrespect in Puah's question turned her stomach into a knot of tangled yarn. Should she tell him the truth? Some of it perhaps, but not all.

"Eliab is the son of an elder."

The intense hatred in Puah's eyes almost sent her racing from the room.

"Is he the heathen you writhe beneath?"

"Be still." She berated Puah as much for her defense as to keep Eliab from striking her tribesman. "How can you speak my father's name in one breath and curse my standing in another? I am untouched. No harm has come to me."

"Liar." Puah's outburst rumbled in his throat. "This is an insult to all our people. We will show no mercy to these thieves. They are a stench to Israel. We will reclaim what is rightfully ours."

She swallowed hard, trying to wet her throat. "Some of the women may be with child. They may choose to stay." It seemed as if Eliab held one of her arms and Puah the other as they tugged in opposing directions. Her friends wanted to stay in this land, and so did she. For Eliab's sake. For her own sake. But she understood the hatred that Puah harbored. She recognized the rage. Her father would possess it as she did once.

"What will Benjamin give us to depart? Dirt?" Puah's taunting laughter filled the small space.

The cloth above her heart trembled with every resounding beat. Witnessing the antics of one so certain of destruction rattled her faith and her hope for forgiveness. "God will not allow you to war against Benjamin."

"He already has. We stand ready to fight."

"We?" Eliab inquired.

"The sons of Joseph stand together." Puah rose higher on his knees and jutted his chest. "The men of Manasseh have raised their swords with ours. Benjamin will never rise from this rubble."

"You speak like a pagan." Words sputtered from her parched lips. "What of our forefather Jacob? Will he not weep on Abraham's bosom when the descendants of Rachel's eldest son murder the remnant of her youngest?"

"A few tears perhaps, but none for the harlots of Shiloh. If you do not return with us, I will spear you once for Caleb and then impale you again for Joab."

In her ear, a high-pitched hum deafened his threat, but she heard her brothers' names as if they had spoken to her from beyond the grave. Squeezing her eyes shut, she prayed for wisdom and the strength to do what was right in God's eyes. If only she knew His will.

She glanced at Eliab. His eyes held a glimmer of fear, questioning if she believed all that Puah shouted as truth. She knew truth from lies. She knew Eliab. She knew him to be a good man, a God-fearing man. And she knew him to be no different than Puah and her brothers.

With a straight back, she strolled closer to Puah and swallowed the hint of vomit in her throat.

"I pity you, Puah. Hatred has you talking like a fool. But I will not see you mistreated. *Shalom.*"

Striding past Eliab and then Ashbanel, she walked to an adjoining room where her soon-to-be father-in-law sat in an overly large chair. She bowed briefly to Berek. In the steadiest voice she could muster, she said, "Do not harm him. He has been a friend to the house of Heriah."

Her request hung in the air, unanswered.

She leaned in closer to her father-in-law. "If you expect mercy from my people, then show some to this spy. Have I not shown compassion beyond measure to your family?"

Berek nodded. "I will heed your concern."

She marched out of the house and into the street.

"Naomi," Eliab called.

She heard his shout, but did not stop, and continued rushing down one alley and another before slumping beside a small pillar of stones.

"Lord, I cannot bear witness to any more death. Do not take my friends from me. Cuzbi feels blessed. Jael is happy here. Spare Isa and Eliab. What have they done to be banished from this land forever? Do they not want to live? Save us, Yahweh. If You are the God of Jacob, then spare Benjamin, the descendants of his son."

The heavens remained quiet except for the song of a locust and the babble of nearby men.

Lifting her eyes to the gray-hued sky, she shouted, "Do You hear me? You must build a fortress around Benjamin. Do not spill any more blood. Not my blood. And not my Eliab's."

18

Naomi rose to her knees and retched like a dog. Her stomach ached from emptying.

Eliab scuffed closer in the twilight.

"I am scared, Eliab. I fear for everyone in this city."

"So do I." He helped her to her feet, grimacing when her weight fell upon his bruised side. "I do not believe God sent you into my arms to have you watch me die by the sword. I know He will protect us."

"How?" She wanted to share his faith, but witnessing Puah's hatred had shattered her confidence. "The elders of Manasseh have sent men to fight with Ephraim. They do not seem concerned for the dancers' future as much as for seeking revenge."

"That is why I must go south into the lands of Judah. Tonight."

"To prepare for another war?" Hope drained from her limbs. She had seen the loss of so many. *Lord, do not take Eliab or my last brother from me.*

"I go to prevent one." He cupped her chin. "The leaders of Ephraim do not want a battle; they want a slaughter. With soldiers from Judah at our side, they may reconsider an attack."

"If only we had gold or silver or cattle to offer Ephraim. They would leave for riches."

"We will prosper someday. Ephraim will have to wait if they desire payment from us for their daughters."

"You share the same vision as Cuzbi." She blinked away tears, thinking of the peril that could befall her friend.

Eliab caressed her shoulder. "I must leave while it is dark. I can be in Bethlehem before the Sabbath."

"Bethlehem? Didn't the Levite travel from there?"

"It is the closest city. Rachel's tomb should remind our brothers of our bond."

She laced her fingers with his. "What makes you so sure my tribe will not overwhelm the city before sundown?"

"The dead would be left unburied." Eliab's voice faltered. "If the high priest is with them, he will not allow the fallen to be eaten by scavengers on our day of rest. If they are alone, I hope they fear the wrath of God should they leave our people to rot in the sun."

Wrapping her arms around his waist, she held him close. Closer than she ever had. "I am going with you. Do not leave me behind. If Puah's words are true, I will be captured and bartered for as a prostitute. With you, I am a voice of reason to Judah. A voice for the girls of Shiloh."

"I cannot." Eliab's back stiffened. "And from what you have told me about your father, he will not allow you to become a harlot."

"I have washed your body and shared your bed. My father has few choices where I am concerned. I saved your life, Eliab. Now you must save mine." She pressed her cheek into his chest. "I will not let you go and chance not seeing you again. The unknown is worse than truth."

Eliab's body softened around her.

She glimpsed, solely for a moment, what being his wife would bring.

"Please do not leave me. I did not leave you on the cliff."

"You are a brave woman, Naomi. How could I chance losing you?" He kissed her forehead. "It is not an easy journey in the dark. We will go together, for I dread returning to find you gone."

"I will not slow you down." She had not had a leisurely life. Her strength would serve her well.

A scrape of sandals drew her attention toward the street. She turned, but she did not separate from Eliab's warmth.

Shadows slipped into the alley. Men's shadows. A couple of broad forms hurried forward in haste.

Eliab stepped in front of her and rested a hand on his blade.

Naomi tensed and readied to strike any attacker. She peeked around Eliab's shoulder and blew out a captive breath.

Ashbanel and Berek approached.

"And what is this display?" Ashbanel quipped.

Eliab faced his half-brother. "We were making plans." Eliab lowered his voice. "To summon the men of Judah."

Berek handed a satchel to Eliab and then began to remove his ornate robe.

"Ride a mule to the east and leave it with the slinger. You must travel on foot to avoid the scouts. Take my garment and my ring. Do not put them on until you reach the city of our brothers in Judah."

Ashbanel rounded on his father. "Eliab is not an elder of Benjamin. I should go in your name."

"If you do not remain in Gibeah, it will arouse suspicion. A leader will be missed, but not a shepherd." Berek folded his cloak and placed it in the leather bag.

"And what about in Bethlehem?" Ashbanel hissed like a steaming pot. "Will they receive a herdsman?"

Even in the dark, Berek's stare could have set a broom tree ablaze. "He is my son and sent by my authority. He speaks for our tribe."

"You trust a son who has not made his woman his wife? I heard her confess as much to that spy. She is not one of us." Ashbanel crossed his arms in self-declared victory.

She cringed at the truth and the disgust in Ashbanel's voice as he spoke it.

"She is a virgin?" Berek beheld Eliab.

"She *is* my wife. We made a vow to wait until after the Sabbath to have a union."

"How can we be sure of her loyalty?" Berek clutched the satchel to his side.

"Because your son and I took an oath." She looked at Eliab and no one else. That strange flutter in her belly fanned her bones. "I would never do anything to harm him. I asked for a betrothal period and he granted my request. Nothing more. Is it not our custom to have a time of waiting?" She cast a glance at Berek, knowing he could not refute her testimony.

Ashbanel stood shoulder to shoulder with his father. "She has no ties to our family since Eliab has failed to make her his own."

Naomi stretched to her full height. "You," she said, pointing at Ashbanel, "may have chosen a wife solely to beget children, but Eliab and I have decided to become known to each other. And out of love we will build this tribe. None of us can give life without God's blessing. Look to Rachel and Sarah. Did they not desire children, only to have God close their wombs until His appointed time? I can wait on God and bond with my husband. Then, and only then, will I beget a child." As she revealed her truth, her heart and breath raced in such an erratic rhythm that she feared a gentle pat would send her careening toward the ground.

Eliab took hold of her hand, gently, but with a firm squeeze.

And in her other hand, Berek placed the satchel containing his robe and his ring.

19

In the thick of darkness, their mule trotted eastward, through the crumbling walls of Gibeah and through barren fields to the house of Berek. Eliab enfolded her in his cloak and shielded her with his body, so she was safe in his lap. He risked the threat of arrows from the hillside.

They snaked an untraceable trail toward home. Neither whispered. To speak in the flatlands invited danger. Tonight she needed her wits. Tonight she would travel farther from Shiloh. Tonight she was the wife of the enemy. Tomorrow she would enter another city that hated Benjamites and ask them to send their sons into battle. One more time. Forgiveness and mercy needed to reign in the hearts of Judah. Two priestly commands she had struggled with herself.

No lamp lit the house of Berek, for the outskirts of the city had little protection. But with so few men to defend it, Gibeah itself had little protection. Her stomach twisted. Would her new home bustle again with life? By appearances, Isa's dwelling stood abandoned, but she knew better. Isa met them at the threshold and disappeared around back with the mule.

She slid inside the half-open door. "Where are the sheep?"

"Scattered," Eliab said in hushed tones. "Their gathering would draw attention to their keeper."

A prickling heat rose from her neck into her

cheeks. "My ewe?"

"Here." Jael tugged her forward.

The odor of damp straw was strong as a small animal brushed her leg. *Yom!* She embraced Jael. "Bless you for sparing them from the wild."

A huffing noise caught Naomi's attention. Cuzbi sauntered toward her.

"That thing has been nibbling my toes."

"Oh, Cuzbi, your complaint I welcome like a song." She reached out for her friend's hand and found it waiting.

"I have spoken to Ashbanel of my condition," Cuzbi whispered. "My husband wishes his heir to survive. We can escape to the hills from here."

What better place for a lethal left-handed slinger? "Your husband will be safe." Naomi hugged her friend. "All of us will."

Eliab tapped her shoulder. "We must leave at once."

"You are going with him?" Jael's breathy squeak sent Yom scurrying toward Cuzbi.

Naomi held Jael's face in her hands. "Eliab will petition for his tribe, but someone needs to speak for the girls of Shiloh. We shouldn't be taken from this land if we wish to stay. The elders in Judah need to know we are content in Gibeah."

Isa settled next to Jael. "You must make Judah understand I have nothing to offer for a bride price. I have loosed the few livestock we found and the land has yet to be planted."

"You could barter for time with Yom." Naomi girded her countenance and breathed deep. "He is unblemished and would fetch a fair price for an offering. But all this talk is for naught if we do not rally

Judah and prevent a massacre. God must provide us with an army to end this matter, and He must send Ephraim and Manasseh back to their lands."

"Hurry on, sister." Cuzbi gave Naomi a gentle shove. "Save your testimony for the elders of Judah. Do I have to push you toward the border?"

Naomi backed toward the door. "Not this time." Before she shuffled out into the darkness, she whispered, "Be safe."

Since neither was mounted on a mule, she jogged to keep up with Eliab's long strides. Her toes pulsed after meeting one too many rocks on the hillsides.

"You are a sure-footed ram on these trails," she whispered.

"Isa and I have searched this way for livestock. I would light a torch, but then every scout and robber would know of our existence. Up ahead is a shortcut to the Camel Road, which will lead us to Jerusalem. Bethlehem will be to the south. It is an easier journey than the cliffs, but there will be travelers. You must put the hood of your cloak up for cover."

"So this time, I am your brother and not your sister?" She deepened her voice.

"I would like others to think that." Eliab lumbered in a manner that would have any bandit thinking twice before an attack.

They walked in silence, prowling past the camps of travelers on the side of the road. After a few hours, they reached the outskirts of Jerusalem and kept going until Bethlehem sat in their sights. Groves lined the mound-like hills. Herds and flocks settled around their shepherds. The occasional oxcart sat on the side of the wide trail, filled with wares for the market.

Eliab led Naomi under two fig trees. The broad

palms blocked the stone silhouette of the city's walls and flat-topped buildings. A rooster crowed, echoing like the summons of a shofar.

Grimacing as he bent to place the satchel near the trunk of the nearest tree, Eliab loosened his belt.

"I need to look like an elder and not like a Bedouin covered in dirt." He turned his back toward her and lifted his tunic.

She glanced away, for in the waning moonlight she could see most of him, and gazing at his form stirred thoughts for which there was no time this night. When enough minutes had passed, she cast a discerning look to see how Berek's robe fit his young son.

"Allow me to straighten the seams." She stepped closer. "Your hem is uneven and a few tassels are splayed. We need you well dressed to impress the elders so an army follows you home."

Eliab watched her take command of his clothing and obeyed her orders to shrug and shift.

"I wish I knew you in Shiloh. You could have sewn all my tunics."

A burst of energy rushed through Naomi's veins. Eliab's praise awoke her tired senses like a cinnamon balm. "You would not have noticed me." She brushed a loose thread. "I did not sit idle much."

"Oh, I would have noticed you. Of that you can be certain." He stilled her hand, kissed it, and went to pack up his satchel.

She hugged her waist and let his kiss dry on her skin. What would she have thought of Eliab if she had seen him with his flocks? He commanded attention with his height, but would that have been enough to interest her? No, not upon itself, but if she were honest, truly honest, his smile and sensitivity would have drawn her like bees to a bloom.

He drew near as if he knew her thoughts. "Rest for a moment. The morning sun will keep you from stubbing your toes."

"I would not have to worry if I knew the landscape."

"It is new for both of us," he said.

His closeness made her think he did not only speak of pathways and pain.

Soon they joined merchants and travelers flooding into Bethlehem. Carts stacked high with food and cages jostled and rattled on the main road into the city. Wares needed to be sold before sundown, before the beginning of the Sabbath. Eliab strutted by the merchants, who slowed their pace to let him pass. Heads turned, but no one reprimanded the stranger who stood a head taller than any man on the march toward town. She took three steps to Eliab's one. The people blurred into a dizzying mass as she rushed to follow Eliab's path.

In the corner of the market square, a man robed in velvet called out to the crowd. Gold rings glistened as his fingers fanned a summons to listen to his speech.

Eliab darted his direction.

The merchant flung his arms out in welcome. "Ah, do you wish to adorn your woman, or yourself?"

She stifled a laugh. She had never seen Eliab covered in gold jewelry, nor could she picture him with nose rings and armbands shearing sheep.

"Not today. I come in search of Sereb, son of Nashon."

The man's grin soured. "Perhaps tomorrow you will barter?"

"Perhaps soon." Eliab glanced her direction.

His confidence emboldened her spirit. She wished for a time of peace. A time when coins jingled in her pouch.

"It is one of your elders I seek at the moment." Eliab's tone held firm to his original request.

The merchant sighed and clicked his tongue at Eliab's refusal to purchase trinkets. "Follow this street up the hill. You will see his house on the right. Two stories."

Eliab thanked the man.

The merchant pushed her aside to flatter a new customer. "Come back with this girl or another."

Her insides twisted like a washrag. Eliab was her betrothed. Try as she had these past days to think of another suitor, or another situation, her thoughts and her feelings stayed loyal to her Benjamite. She would not step aside and let someone else be Eliab's wife. She would not be forced by Judah, or anyone, to return to her parents.

She grabbed his hand discreetly as they neared the crest of the hill. His fingers were uncommonly cool for the desert air, but his grip held firm.

Eliab halted in front of the elder's house. "I thought your touch would calm my heart but it runs like a rabbit."

"We should pray," she said, wanting to embrace him but respectful of the people shuffling by. "Though I am confident you can speak as well as your father."

"I do not fear speaking on behalf of Benjamin, but I do fear burying the rest of my family. I do not know if I have the strength to return to another graveyard."

She wrapped his hand in both of hers. "The tribe of Judah will come to Benjamin's rescue. You told me once that you prayed the night of the raid for God to send you a wife. He did, Eliab. I tried to hate you, but I cannot. I meant what I said to your father. God has a plan, and I do not believe it ends here."

He swept a piece of hair under her head covering. "Then let us ask Him to reveal it." Eliab bowed his head. "Give me Your wisdom to speak, O Lord. Open the hearts of the elders to our plea. May Rachel not weep for her descendants in the bosom of Abraham."

"Hear us, O God," she echoed.

Was it her imagination, or did the commotion on the streets hush during their petition? She would take anything—the warmth on her face, their safe travels, the merchant's knowledge, anything—as a sign that God was with them.

Eliab knocked on the door of the cream-colored stone dwelling. The hollow sound of knuckles on wood echoed down the street.

Please acknowledge us. Energy surged in her veins even though she stood still as a sculpture.

The door opened. A servant occupied the entry and assessed Eliab's robe and stature.

"I come to speak with Sereb as a fellow elder." Eliab's official tone sent the woman into a head-bobbing bow.

The servant invited them inside.

Naomi stifled a sigh of relief.

"I will see if my master is able to visit. My mistress is awake. And I will send for water for your feet."

Naomi bent at the knees to hide her sandals. Traveling in the dark had not been kind to her toes. Her stomach rumbled at the aroma of bread baking. When harvest came to East Gibeah, she would bake enough food to feed an army of strangers.

Footsteps clapped on the floor. A woman appeared dressed in the color of honey and jeweled with pure malachite.

"My husband has just risen. May I offer you refreshment while you wait?" She clasped her hands at her waist.

"Thank you," Eliab said. "I come with an urgent request for Judah's elders. My father spoke highly of your husband and his influence. I hope we can discuss a plan of action."

The woman's face brightened with a pride-filled smile. "My husband is well respected in this city and beyond its walls."

"As I have heard. The tribe of Benjamin is in need of his—"

"You are a Benjamite?" The woman's smile vanished. Her jaw gaped as she crumpled to the floor.

Did she faint? Naomi rushed to her aid as did the servant who carried the washbasin.

"Murderer," Sereb's wife screamed. "Get out. Get your evil out of my house." The woman shook her clenched fists at Eliab. "Husband, come quickly."

Naomi fell to her knees to beseech the woman. "We come for aid. For peace."

"Liar. Sin reigns in Gibeah." The woman's gaze grew savage. Spit struck Naomi's cheek. The woman flailed her arms and lunged at Naomi with talon-like hands, ripping at Naomi's head covering and the hair underneath.

Scalp on fire, Naomi pried her ringlets from the woman's clenched fists. Naomi stumbled backward from the force of her own pull.

"Calm her," Eliab ordered the servants.

O Lord, did I appear as ugly with wrath as this

woman?

Two girls and a boy struggled to raise their mistress.

A man swooped into the room with his turban askew and his robe barely closed. He caught the woman in a husbandly embrace.

"What is the meaning of this outburst?"

Naomi's bones rattled at Sereb's indignation. She jumped toward Eliab and closer to the door.

Eliab held open his hands and dipped in a show of respect. "I am Eliab *ben* Berek. I come as an elder from Benjamin, seeking an army to keep us from ruin."

"And you came to Judah? Did you not slaughter our men? Kill my son?" Sereb's voice cracked. His wife sobbed uncontrollably.

"We face annihilation on your counsel." Eliab lowered to one knee. "I beg of you, as a fellow son of Jacob, listen to our plea. Help us."

Sereb shook his head with violent swings that threatened to send his turban across the room.

"You have come to blame Judah for your problems. Our people's blood is on Benjamin's hands. Alone." Sereb hurled a cup at Eliab.

Eliab ducked.

Naomi snatched the well-aimed pottery before it hit the wall and shattered.

"Leave us. Now." Sereb readied more ammunition. "Take your pagan whore with you."

Eliab grasped her arm.

"No. Leave me be." Naomi held her ground and faced Sereb. "I am not a heathen." Her throat blazed as she controlled her rage. "I am a daughter of Ephraim. I serve the Most High God. Do not turn us away because of the past. Can we not discuss the future of our people?"

Sereb's wife aimed a vase at Naomi's face. "You dare to address my husband, you vile girl."

Naomi readied her own cup to launch. "I came seeking mercy from your household so Rachel would not weep for her descendants. But I can see there is no justice here."

At Eliab's urging, Naomi dropped her cup, turned, and fled.

High-pitched wailing and the smashing of stoneware followed in their wake.

20

Eliab stormed through the marketplace. Vendors waved at him and offered a taste of almonds and olives, but he did not stop his limp-legged march. Naomi drew alongside him and tapped his arm.

"We will not leave Bethlehem until we have sought every elder. All we need is one ally to rally some fighting men."

"I should have anticipated the hatred." He slowed and paced next to a wagon. "I thought the leaders would forgive those who remained alive."

"They are wounded men." She tried to strengthen Eliab's spirit after the conflict with Sereb and his wife. "Did I not have the same disgust when you captured me?"

He shook his head. "You panicked when I took you from Shiloh, and you were mad, but in everything, I saw a compassion that not only comforted Jael—it challenged me to be a better man." He towered over her, blocking the sun.

"I know you as a man who follows God's laws. A remnant of good from evil."

"And?" His voice grew harsh.

"A laborer as well as a leader."

"And?"

His drawn and creased face concerned her. Had he lost confidence in himself?

She placed a hand on his robe. "You are a man

who makes me feel things I cannot put into words, much less demonstrate in a public market."

His chest sank like a sack of grain emptying into a trough. "Why does God give me a wife if it is not meant to be?"

She tugged on a twisted tassel. "Sereb may be against us, but there are other leaders in this city. We need only find one elder willing to fight for his brothers' survival."

"Then let us go to the courtyard, for any elder worth his station will be making his way to morning prayer."

"I hope God has a listening ear," Naomi said. "I have enough petitions for the whole city."

Eliab cinched his belt. He scanned the crowd before bending down. "When our task is finished," he whispered, "we must talk about those feelings you have, for I believe you caught them from me. And tomorrow, after the Sabbath, we are free to act upon them." His half-hearted wink made her float on air in the midst of the bustle of the barterers.

They crossed to the north side of the city, the direction facing her home in Shiloh. Days ago, she would have lunged off these city walls and fled to her tribe, but not anymore. If only her father and brother knew of her change of heart.

Chairs sat in a semicircle at the edge of a clearing overlooking the fields and flocks surrounding Bethlehem of Judah. This had to be the place of prayer, for a canopy covered the elders' small thrones. The masses would stand in the open, braving the brunt of the sun.

Eliab surveyed some men talking in a distant alley. "At least no one has come to stone me."

"Do not even utter those words." She shuddered at the mention of violence.

Women shuffled by with vessels of water and set them near the chairs.

Naomi followed the procession and beckoned Eliab to come and wait near the tall cleansing jars. Amongst a crowd they would not be noticed.

"You are early."

Naomi startled at the voice. She whipped around, heart thudding, and beheld an elderly man half the size of Eliab. The man's crooked neck and hunched shoulders did not aid his stature. He wore no shoes. His tunic, though thick and sewn straight, held no adornments. Due to his stoop, his gray hair hung forward in his face. Poor man. How sad to be a servant at his age.

"We came early for prayer." Eliab's shoulders dipped. "I've traveled to see the elders of Judah."

The servant waved off Eliab's comment. "We must get ready. No one is in a hurry this day." The man beckoned Eliab and her with his hand. "Come, help me arrange the area for ceremonial washing."

Eliab hesitated, but she pushed him forward. "Can you lift the vessels?" she asked, remembering his injured arm.

He scowled. "Women carried those."

"I know, but they did not fall off a cliff onto their side."

The servant hobbled her direction. "Young woman, follow me."

Eliab settled a jar on his shoulder and motioned for her to go with the man. The servant handed out tasks like sweet cakes.

The old man pointed to the side of the courtyard.

"The small jugs go on the end. Bring the cups as well." Apparently, he had confidence in her fetching, for he left her alone and trailed after Eliab, making him shift and position the tall jars to his liking. Eliab's patience with the servant lifted her spirits. She longed to see him interact with children. Their own children. *Lord, bless us with a kind ear in Judah.*

Men, women, and children arrived for prayer. Eliab knelt in a line in the front of the courtyard with the other men. His brightly hued robe shone like a jewel among the muted colors and plain weaves of the worshippers' garments. Sitting in the back of the crowd, she nestled beside a lady large enough to shield her from any flying ceremonial cups.

Two men not much older than her father and dressed in flowing robes arrived. The crowd hung back as the prominent men poured water over each other's hands. They sauntered toward the wooden thrones and set themselves apart from the crowd. Neither scanned the courtyard for a tall Benjamite. *Toda raba.* Thanks be to God.

Her breath hitched when Sereb appeared among a mass of townspeople. Attendants ushered his wife to a stool not far from where the last row of men gathered. Naomi instinctively brushed a hand over her head, her scalp still tender from the woman's attack.

Sereb washed, but as he turned to join his fellow elders for prayer and the reading of the Law, his chest broadened as if he inhaled the wind.

"You." He jabbed a finger over and over at Eliab. "Why does a dog from Benjamin seek counsel with Judah? Did you not turn your back on God and the other sons of Jacob?"

Naomi tensed. She ducked behind her broad

neighbor and scanned the perimeter for anything to use as a weapon.

The muttering of worshippers hummed like a swarm of locusts.

Eliab held up his hands. He dipped his head in reverence. "I come in peace. To ask a favor for Jacob's descendants."

Strangers pushed Eliab as if to remove him from the courtyard. He stumbled, but the crush of men kept his body upright.

Her heart lodged in her throat. If harm came to Eliab, what would become of Cuzbi and Jael? "Send us Your angels, Lord," she muttered. The lady beside her scowled like the prayer distracted from the commotion.

The elderly servant waddled right by her post.

"Leave him be," the old man shouted. He elbowed people who did not clear from his path.

She echoed his request in hopes others would join in. No one did.

Jabbing a crooked finger at Sereb, the servant continued ranting. "He is a visitor to our land. An elder. Where is your hospitality?"

Sereb's face grew scarlet as if he was flushed from too much wine. "This traitor is not welcome in Judah."

"Why not?" The words rushed from Naomi's lips. "Is he not an Israelite?" She moved closer to her elderly ally and hoped he had a household that would come to his aid.

"Sereb, bring order." The booming request sent a shiver of relief down her spine.

The crowd hushed their debate.

A man, broader than most, his collar adorned with polished bronze rings, shoved forward and stood next to Eliab. With his size, only a fool would challenge the newcomer.

"You insult a guest and a fellow worshipper." The fierce-looking stranger crossed his arms over his chest.

Sereb widened his stance and positioned himself in the front of the courtyard. "What concern is he of yours, Onan?"

"It appears I owe a debt to this foreigner, who arranged our vessels in your absence." Onan clapped a hand on Eliab's good shoulder. "I wish to listen to his reasons for disturbing us."

Was this the servant's master? Whoever he was, she welcomed his defense of her husband. Husband? She yearned for a time when people would accept their joining without passing judgment.

"He brings war to our gates." Sereb made sure every person within blocks of the courtyard heard his accusation. "He is sent by the leaders of Benjamin to amass an army. I, for one, have lost enough sons in Gibeah. But then, you thirst for a fight, don't you?"

Onan chuckled, deep and taunting. "No, brother, you misunderstand me. I don't run into battle, but I do not run from them."

"My desire is to prevent a slaughter, to prevent a war." Eliab beseeched both elders equally. "The fighting men of Ephraim and Manasseh threaten to destroy what is left of Benjamin. They seek revenge for the daughters we took as wives."

"See." Sereb strung out his accusation. "They caused men to break a holy vow made by the tribal leaders."

"We did no such thing," Eliab's voice boomed, rising above Sereb's shade tent. "We kept the fathers of Ephraim innocent of wrongdoing. They did not give us the girls. We stole the virgins to keep their fathers blameless."

Gasps skittered among the gatherers.

Naomi edged forward. If the crowd became hostile, she would need Onan to come to her and Eliab's defense.

Onan clapped his hands to stop the gossiping. He turned to address Eliab.

"Why do you come to Judah in search of fighting men and not to our brothers, Reuben or Gad?"

Eliab surveyed the crowd as if choosing an army. "Berek, my father and an elder in his own right, claims it was at Judah's urging that we lay in wait in Shiloh and grabbed the daughters of Ephraim when they came out to dance."

Sereb waved his hands as if dismissing Eliab. "False accusations."

"My father would not lie." Eliab's shoulders snapped back as if he was ready to strike Sereb. "Elders from Judah told my father to go to the feast in Shiloh."

"Onan, dismiss this babble. What elder in Judah would encourage such insult? We are not fools." Sereb settled onto his wooden throne.

The crooked-back servant brushed by her without a glance and grabbed Onan's braided belt. "Son, do not pass judgment on the Benjamite."

Son?

"Why not?" Onan questioned.

The old servant pulled on his tapered beard. "For it may have come from my lips."

"My father insisted the plan came from an elder of Judah," Eliab said.

Onan straightened. "My father-in-law, Hamul, is

an elder of Judah."

The gray-haired elder scuffled toward Sereb. "I have not broken any laws," Hamul stammered. "I planted the seed for a new beginning and my idea bore fruit for this Benjamite. He took a dancer and has found a wife." Her former taskmaster turned and pointed at her. "She is here among us."

Gasps and mutterings swept through the courtyard. Bystanders moved in unison to gawk at her, the stolen dancer.

Sweat trickled down the side of her face. She tried to smile, but her lips quivered, and she feared she resembled a braying donkey.

"Is this Benjamite your husband?" Onan asked, loud enough for all of Bethlehem to hear.

If she wanted to go home, home to stay, this was her chance, for she stood among elders of one of Israel's tribes, and they would see to her safe return. Tears welled in her eyes. Her past evaporated like water in the desert, but her future brightened before her eyes. A future of her own choosing with a man she desired.

What would her family say if they heard her declaration? Would they want to see her if they knew she had testified to being a Benjamite's wife? Would they acknowledge her children? Eliab's seed?

She envisioned the campfire in Shiloh, the booths, the girls. If Eliab sat before her, would she have given him her attention? She had never met anyone like Eliab. And she never would again, for he had spoiled her for another man. No man could take his place in her heart.

A stuttered breath shook her whole being. Naomi swallowed the lump choking her throat. "He is my husband."

Her gaze met Eliab's. He joined her, taking her hand in a show of support.

A desire deep in her gut filled her with hope and calmed her racing heart. "I once was an Ephraimite, but now I am a wife of a Benjamite, and I beg you to save my people from destruction." She looked over the women huddled around her. "Let us pray for Benjamin and no more bloodshed."

"Unless it's a Benjamite's," a man shouted.

Something hard struck her cheek. A stone dropped to the ground as pain radiated through her jaw.

Eliab pulled her behind him. Onan and Hamul flanked his sides.

"These visitors are under my protection," Onan bellowed.

Holding her face, she began to pray, "Hear, O Israel. The Lord is our God. The Lord alone."

Thankfully, those around her joined in reciting the Shema. Onan's deep voice wailed loudest.

Sereb, who had flown off his chair, had to stop and finish the prayer.

"Love the Lord your God with all your heart, with all your soul, and with all your might."

Naomi closed her eyes to keep from weeping, for a young shepherd and a younger weaver had finally found an ally from the tribe of Judah.

21

Onan led her, Eliab, and a procession of elders to his domain. She prayed Onan would be able to convince the other leaders to send an army to Gibeah and answer Berek's call.

A woman, not as tall as Cuzbi but dressed in fine tapestry with gold bracelets to spare, shadowed Naomi's every step. She glanced to see if the woman held rocks. Her jaw ached from the pelt in the courtyard.

"So you are with the Benjamite that brings another war to my doorstep?" The woman matched Naomi's stride, turned, and walked with her back to the men.

The hair on Naomi's arms rose as if carded. Would this woman attack her like Sereb's wife? She clenched her fists to ward off an assault.

"There will not be a battle if Judah comes and speaks for Benjamin." Naomi's cheeks grew warm. Where was the compassion for the weak? How many times did she and Eliab have to beg for help? "We need the tribes from the north to think Judah will fight on our behalf. They will expect Judah to remain true to its reputation as having the best warriors." Naomi's voice quivered as she thought of Jael and Cuzbi hidden in Isa's dwelling. "I am tired of mourning the dead. This time, we may save lives and a remnant in Benjamin."

The woman grabbed Naomi's hand.

Naomi flinched. She cast a glance at Eliab, but he

was deep in conversation.

"Do not be afraid," the woman said. "Follow me around to the side of the house. My servants will need water to wash all these regal feet." She tugged Naomi into an alley and led her through a courtyard and a set of wooden doors. Crossing the threshold, the woman called out instructions to two girls sweeping the entry.

"You are Onan's wife?" Naomi asked, catching her breath from the unplanned dash.

"And Hamul's daughter, Abigail. You met my father this morning. It seems he is to blame for the schemes in Shiloh."

Abigail sauntered down a hallway and paraded into the living room.

Onan greeted his wife.

Young girls with hair as black as Abigail's came with jugs of water to assist the servants in washing the feet of the elders.

Naomi stayed in the hall. Her heart could not take another confrontation with Sereb.

Eliab sought her out. "You are safe here. Onan understands what we need." He swept a thumb under her cheekbone and scowled when he inspected the skin below her brow. "I will not let you be struck again."

She knew Eliab meant well, but he was one man against many. No matter how much he desired to, he could not protect her from all harm. She stilled his hand. "I will heal as you are healing. Now you must convince the elders to give us an army and we can go back to East Gibeah and be safe in our own home."

"I shall do my best for God and for you." Hidden from view, he casually caressed her arm. "Seeing Onan and his family makes me want to start my own."

His touch was like a drink of cool water soothing

her stomach and enlivening her soul. She tucked the lingering sensation into her memory. Soon he would not have to stop after one stroke. "We will be together when Gibeah is safe and my tribe returns to their fields."

"I will hold you to your word." Eliab turned and joined the elders.

What would her wedding night be like? Her mother was not near to prepare her for marriage. And she did not want an encounter like Cuzbi's.

The slap of sandals brought her back to the trouble at hand.

Abigail approached. "I do not know what possessed my father to send the Benjamites into Ephraim's vineyards, but the deception does not seem to have cast empty nets." Abigail raised her sculpted black eyebrows. "Unless there is a vengeful betrothed lying wait beyond Gibeah's borders, it would seem you are content with your husband."

Naomi shook her head and then thought better of it as pain settled into her cheek. "My father had not arranged a marriage. And I know of two other girls content to stay with their Benjamites…I mean, husbands."

"Perhaps my father isn't as foolish as others say. You spoke forthright during prayer and that kind of strength comes from the heart."

And fright. "I spoke my story."

"Indeed." Abigail ushered Naomi into a room for cooking. "Help me with this bread. Sundown on the Sabbath waits for no woman. And we will have soldiers to feed."

"Then you believe Onan will raise an army?" Naomi sat beside a basket of flour and measured grain, thankful for the privacy of the side walls and the view of the clear sky.

"That is to be seen, but my husband is headstrong, and I can tell he is considering your cause." Abigail called to her daughters while she placed a stone on the fire.

When the girls arrived, Abigail set them to the chore of baking bread and motioned for Naomi to follow. Slipping off her sandals, Abigail indicated for Naomi to do the same.

"Come with me," Abigail said with a tug on Naomi's sleeve.

Naomi tensed as they passed the elders' meeting room. Sereb's ranting, though muffled, brought back visions of flying pottery.

Abigail eased open a door. "It is a small pantry," she whispered. "If we press our ears to the stone, we can hear the discussion."

"Is this not dishonest?" What would Onan or Eliab say if they caught them eavesdropping?

Abigail pushed Naomi forward. "I accept that my husband fights for Judah, but I do not want to be caught unaware. I need time to meditate on his decisions."

A basket of bean pods took up the corner, so Naomi wedged herself close to the wall and inwardly welcomed the flow of words seeping through the stone.

Sereb's accusations came forth.

"How do I know the men left in Gibeah have repented of their vile ways? My people fought bravely for two days before God gave us victory. We suffered more than most tribes."

"My father upholds the laws of Moses." Eliab's

voice held steady. "The remnant in Gibeah follows God's commandments."

"But your father ruled Benjamin before the war?"

Naomi stiffened at Onan's questioning of Berek's authority. She prayed for Eliab to remain calm.

"Yes, and he tried to rid the city of false gods. Too many men had turned from the truth. We are not the first tribe to be overrun with idols."

"And you won't be the last," Onan remarked. "Have we not struggled with foreigners bringing images of their gods into Bethlehem?"

"Nonsense," Sereb shouted louder than a ram's horn. She and Abigail drew back from the wall. "Our elders have stayed true to our ways and our God."

"Fool, we are not perfect." Hamul must have been pacing, for his chastisement waned, then grew louder. "The oath our people took left Benjamin with no hope of wives."

"That is why you recommended stealing the virgins?" The question came from an unknown elder.

"What better way around the vow than to steal?" Hamul's answer held no hint of humor.

"Well, they are not virgins now," someone said.

"Judah will not pay one shekel of a bride price to Ephraim. The women are worth nothing."

Abigail shook her head at Sereb's statement. Naomi balled a fist, wishing she could strike Sereb for his insult.

"The women are worth everything."

She knew that voice. A flutter of pride filled her chest.

"The girls of Shiloh are our wives. Some are with child by now. We cannot send them back to face a life of shame. They are part of our families."

"Only a harlot would accept a union with a Benjamite."

"Sereb!" Onan snapped.

Naomi covered her mouth lest she answer through the wall. Abigail stroked Naomi's arm. Her wide eyes showed her disbelief at the insult.

"My wife is as honorable as any woman in Judah. She did not rush into my bed. You heard her plea for forgiveness in the place of prayer. She is a godly woman who prays for peace."

Eliab's praise whipped her heart into a frenzy. She worried the men would hear the pounding and discover her hiding place.

"Who are we to decide this matter? Shall we not seek the high priest?" a stranger asked.

"We have no time." Eliab's tone grew urgent. "Send an envoy north, and when they return, Benjamin will be destroyed. A distant memory."

"A bad one."

Could Sereb not reason for the good of Abraham's descendants for one moment?

A stomp echoed through the meeting room.

"I will raise an army to protect Gibeah." No fear of fight rang in Onan's declaration. Naomi glanced at Abigail. Onan's wife rested her forehead against the stone, her mouth mumbling a petition to God.

"You may ride out to my kin, but I will stay here."

At least they had some support.

"I will not spill one more drop of my family's blood for Benjamin. We have sacrificed too many."

So have I, Sereb. So have we all.

"Then Judah rides out divided," an elder declared.

Raucous conversation rose from the room.

Abigail motioned for Naomi to leave their hideout.

They put on their sandals and returned to the fire. Abigail sent her daughters for more water.

Naomi returned to making flatbread like any other day, except this day would never leave her memory.

She handed some dough to Abigail. "Are you upset that Onan has thrown in his lot with Benjamin?"

"I married a warrior." No emotion showed on Abigail's face. Not a glimmer of pride. Not a tear of sadness. "I pray that his skill brings him back to me." Abigail regarded her while testing the bread. "And your husband? Does he follow our God as he confessed?"

Naomi shifted her weight. Was Abigail insinuating Eliab had lied about his father and his tribe? She beheld Abigail's gaze. This woman needed to know that Onan and Hamul fought for good, and for good people.

"My husband is an honorable man. He was away from the city when the Levite's companion was attacked."

Abigail stopped cooking. "How do you know he would not have participated in the offense had his plans not taken him away from his family?"

How honest should she be with Abigail? Would Eliab want her to speak of their vow? He had praised her for not rushing into his bed, but he did not reveal that all they had done in his bed was sleep. So far. Was Eliab afraid the elders would take her from him? Could she be as coy as Eliab in her testimony? She swallowed hard.

"I know my husband is trustworthy because he let me keep something valuable that was in his interest to take."

Abigail tapped her arm. "Keep working and tell

me."

Naomi's temples pulsed. She inspected the dough. "Um."

"Mother." A young man entered the room from the alley, his arms filled with wood. "Do you have need of kindling?"

Naomi blew out a breath, thankful for the interruption.

"Yes, yes. But do not travel far." Abigail handed her son a piece of bread and returned to her task. "And this gift, Naomi?" Abigail cocked her head and popped a piece of manna in her mouth.

Naomi's eyes widened. She wanted Abigail to think she and Eliab had become one. That she could possibly be with child. That a family in Benjamin was worth the fight. She had to deny her new friend the truth, for she would not risk being returned to her father to appease Judah. Think. Think. Think. "The possession was…a ewe about to give birth. What shepherd gives away two animals when he slaves to find but one?" She placed her dough on the stone with a slightly unsteady hand and measured more grain.

"Then there is hope for Benjamin. For before, they would not have denied themselves anything."

Naomi poured water into her bowl. What had Eliab really denied her? Her freedom at first, but then he had set her free from bondage to the Moabite. He gave her the ewe at Isa's ridicule. He gave her the loom that stood in their bedroom. He gave her the truth about his betrothal to the Reubenite. He had not held back anything except what mattered most to him. And to her.

"You have a paste in that bowl," Abigail said.

Naomi snapped out of her daydream. "You are

right. I am weary from traveling, but that is of little consequence when we have men to feed. We will need many men if Benjamin is to have a future."

Footsteps echoed in the house.

Abigail stood. Naomi followed her into the hall.

Sereb and a half-dozen elders strode from the dwelling in haste.

Abigail bowed before entering the meeting room. With a show of respect, Naomi knelt in the doorway.

"Are they going to ready their kin?" Abigail cast a knowing glance at Naomi.

Onan went to his wife. "Amram will speak to his family, but he will not ride with us. Your father and I will represent Judah."

"How many men will follow your lead?" Eliab's voice rasped from the burden he shouldered for Benjamin.

Onan tightened his belt. His bronze adornments sparkled even though no light shone in on him. "A few hundred. Maybe more if I am convincing."

Hundreds? Where was the lion of Judah? But more importantly, where was God?

"In a few hours the Sabbath is upon us." Eliab laced his hands as if to pray. "We have a city and countryside to cover."

Hamul reared up like his hunched back had miraculously straightened. "Was our judge Gideon not victorious against thousands with barely three hundred men?"

Naomi jumped to her feet. Her knees barely held her upright. This day had whipped her hopes like wind on a torn sail. "Hamul, an angel of the Lord appeared to the judge of which you speak. We have not received a messenger from God like Gideon."

Hamul hobbled toward her and pointed his crooked finger at the heavens.

"Not yet, woman. Not yet."

22

Naomi peered at the evening sky from a window in Onan's guest room.

Eliab rested a hand on her hip and pulled her into his chest. "How many stars do you see?"

"Two." Her throat grew thick like a soaked reed. "Another day and our Sabbath will be over."

"Ah, three stars." Eliab pointed above the neighbor's roof. "We have to fight, Naomi. So be it. If God wills that I go to my death, I will go. But I have been in earnest prayer that we will be spared another slaughter." He hesitated, breathing as if the air became heavy. "My one regret is that I have not been a true husband to you." His arms cinched around her waist. "Though do not be mistaken—I count you as my wife. I love you, daughter of Heriah. Lord willing, I will show you how much very soon." His wisp of a touch along her face nearly buckled her knees.

She turned in his arms.

He bent to kiss her.

She wanted this kiss. She wanted a chance to show him that their time together was not a mistake, not chance. They had been brought together for more than just a bedding and babies. Lacing her fingers behind his neck, she took hold and pressed her lips to his. He seized her mouth hard and fast. A powerful sensation coiled like a tendril from her toes to her belly, all the way to her breasts. Breaking free for air, she held on to him and breathed into his chest.

"If God is with us, perhaps you will not have to wait much past tomorrow's eve to truly become my husband."

"And if He is not?" Eliab bent so they were face to face. His gaze grew serious. "If something should happen to me, find your father or your brother and return to your family."

Naomi closed her eyes to keep tears from spilling onto her cheeks. If she were returned to her family, it would mean Eliab had perished. *God, I beg of You, send us Your angels.* She took hold of Eliab's hand and hoped he did not feel the drumming of her pulse. "The tribal elders will listen to you and Onan. They will see the wisdom in leaving their daughters as wives so a tribe of Jacob can remain in this land."

Eliab's brow furrowed as if the weight of their journey rested there. "I have my father's robe and gold ring, but it did not persuade more than four hundred men to answer our call. Perhaps if my father had spoken, more would have joined us."

"I do not believe so." She made sure his brown eyes beheld her own. "You speak the truth with boldness."

"You cannot know this."

"I know you." She kept Abigail's listening room a secret. "And that is all I need to know. Now, you must rest this morning and noonday before you and I strap on a sword and meet Onan and his men to travel the Camel Road. After sundown. As *one*." She emphasized her last word.

"Naomi, I—"

"Shh." She placed a finger over his lips. "I told you before—we journey together. Do not hide me away in the straw of a cart, or with the animals. I am a Benjamite now and your wife, Eliab. You told me before—God sent me into your arms. Do not send me away."

"How can I argue with myself and with our God?" He pressed a kiss to her forehead. "I am going to trust that there has been enough blood spilled in Gibeah."

When another sun had set, Eliab dressed for battle. She followed him into the bustle on the road leading to Gibeah. Torches lit the Camel Road. Their flames illuminated the sandstone hills, casting shadows upon crags. The landscape filled with eerie shapes, eyes of black that watched soldiers lining up for war. Not just war, but a much-needed victory.

Soldiers nodded in acknowledgement of Eliab as they passed by. Some men laughed and skirmished with swords, advancing on one another like doing battle was a day in the fields picking the harvest. Leather breastplates and sheaves, swords, shields, and slings accompanied everyone who had heeded Onan's charge. Their garrison of weapons outshone all she had seen among her tribe. The divisions of Judah made a fearful sight.

During the Sabbath, she had repeated prayers over and over for protection, but most of all for peace. Onan and Eliab had remained apart during the Sabbath, their time of rest, lest they plan defenses or a rescue of the city and thus anger God.

Hurry, Judah. For Ephraim may not wait until morning.

Onan, Hamul, and another elder sat upon horses whose bridles and blankets were studded with polished bronze rings and baubles. A vacant mount waited on the end. Only one.

Eliab crossed his arms. Whether by chance or by reason, his ring of authority shone in the torchlight. "My wife will need a mount. She must not leave my sight."

Naomi squinted at the rows of men. She stood as a child at their waists with no armor or fierce weapon. A shiver pimpled her skin. *Lord, spare us from battle.*

Hamul trotted his horse mere feet from where she stood. "I am in agreement. She is the reason we go to Gibeah, is she not?"

"Father, you are the reason we go to Gibeah." Onan motioned for Eliab to mount. A mule was brought forward. "Let her ride. She will be safe with us. The scouts will warn us of danger."

The soldier bringing her mount stood taller and two hands wider than Eliab. His breastplate shone like fine polished silver in the dense light. A helmet covered his forehead, nose, and cheeks. She had never seen a stabbing sword as long and ornate as the one attached to this warrior's hip. Naomi's scalp tingled like she had lain on an anthill.

"You are Naomi *bat* Heriah?" The man's voice was definite but not harsh.

She nodded. Did the men know of her kidnapping from Shiloh?

"Thank you for bringing me an animal to ride."

The soldier held her mule while she mounted. Light trade winds chilled her face as she glanced at the dark tunnel of road that lay ahead. She followed Eliab, lingering a few paces behind the elders.

The slap of sandals echoed above the trail and off the cliffs as the men of Judah marched at a determined pace. No chatter rang out. No prayers. Only steadfast stomps and silence.

Nearing the outskirts of Gibeah where she and Eliab had angled through the hills down to the road, a scout galloped toward the row of elders. The rider pulled the reins taut, causing dust to swirl into the shadowed air.

"We have discovered a Benjamite and some women in a crag up ahead."

Her heart raced faster than the spy's mount. Had these people fled fighting? Had Ephraim and Manasseh not waited until morning to start their siege? Her chest grew tight at the thought of her friends hiding in Isa's small dwelling.

"Bring them to us," Onan said. "I will not carry on into an ambush."

Eliab stiffened as if blame was cast on his honor. "I will talk to my tribesman."

"As you wish," Onan replied. "They can prepare us for what lies ahead."

In the dim of the torchlight, horses trotted forward. Sounds of a scuffle came from the rear of the scouting party.

"Get your fingers off me, or I will bite and swallow them. I am an elder's wife, not a harlot." The voice carried too far for a warring party.

Cuzbi! Tears of relief pressed against Naomi's eyelids.

"I know that woman." Naomi sprang from her mule and sprinted toward the struggle. "She is from Shiloh."

"Where have you been?" Cuzbi raged. She slapped at the air as if clearing a swarm of flies. "Our home is no more. They have burnt everything but the rock."

23

Hope drained from Naomi's soul. Were they really too late? Had Ephraim attacked before the Sabbath ended? Was Benjamin no more? Had the remainder of Eliab's family been slain?

My family.

She grabbed hold of Cuzbi's mount to steady herself.

"What of your husband, Ashbanel, and Berek?" Her voice trembled and squeaked as she listed those who may have perished.

Eliab closed the distance between the elders and the scouts with three long strides. He positioned himself behind her.

"What of my father? The city? Tell me." Eliab's voice climbed as high as the cliffs. An eerie quiet settled over the small crowd of leaders. Did they wait to see if they should press on or mourn the slaughtered?

"Spies attacked East Gibeah, but we are safe," a man shouted. "The city awaits a siege. Your father and Ashbanel are barricaded inside."

Naomi knew that sharp cadence to be Isa's. His announcement warmed her bones like a sun-drenched woolen blanket.

The scouts parted for a rider to come through. A soldier rode forward, leading a mount whose back bore Isa and Jael.

Eliab practically pulled Isa from atop the horse with his embrace.

Jael cuddled Yom to her chest. "We were blessed to make it to the hills, Naomi."

"Praise Yahweh." Naomi blew out a pent-up breath.

"They can see we made it to the hills." Cuzbi righted herself on her mount. "I was trying to explain what happened when Naomi started wailing."

"How did you keep the women safe?" Eliab remained at Isa's side.

"Many buildings outside of Gibeah have been burned. When I saw a few raiders approaching, I sent the women toward the cliffs. One raider broke off to follow. Now he can only crawl."

Naomi cringed at what might have happened to Jael and Cuzbi had Isa not been a skilled slinger. Her chest grew tight. She prayed the man maimed was not her brother. She had already lost two brothers to slingers. The killing needed to end.

Isa glanced up as if he just noticed the elders of Judah. "Camps of fighting men are all around the city. Our men are stationed by the old walls, but with the gaps and rubble, they cannot keep the other tribes from advancing."

Onan dismounted and paced in front of the elders, scouts, and Isa. His bronze-adorned breastplate quaked with every footstep. "If Gibeah is surrounded as you say, then Ephraim and Manasseh have brought a force, for they would not leave the high ground unprotected. We must divide our men and feign a larger number."

Onan had been known to Naomi for only two days, but his confidence soothed her anxiety like a drink of warm goat's milk.

"How many divisions has Judah brought?" Isa asked.

"We number four hundred." Onan announced the number with pride.

"What?" Isa and Cuzbi chorused their surprise.

"Our soldiers are worth three of any other." No one dared to disagree with Onan's assessment.

Eliab clapped Isa's shoulder. "We owe a debt to Onan that we were able to round up these men. Other elders insulted Benjamin and cared not that we may be wiped from this land."

Naomi stood in the dark with an uncertain future before her like the night Eliab swept her onto his mule and away from her home. Had she not prayed for God's protection? Had God not kept her safe? Had He not performed a miracle in her heart? How could she calm the fear of the people she loved?

She stepped to Onan's side.

"Have all of us not prayed and asked for God's guidance? We have offered Him our best sacrifices. Our best gifts. Why would He abandon us now?" Eliab nodded in agreement. She looked to Cuzbi and Jael. "I do not know why I am here on a dark road leading to war, but I do not want to be anywhere else." Love swelled her heart so big she thought it would burst through her rib cage. "We came here as daughters of Ephraim, but now we are wives of Benjamites. Our homes can be rebuilt. Let us go and save our people. God can give us a victory."

"My wife speaks for me as well." Eliab joined her. "Let us plan our siege and not lose heart. We need to position our men before sunrise and be ready to reason with the elders of the tribes face to face."

"Is there no one else to come to our aid?" Cuzbi did not seem impressed with Onan's prowess. "I thought Eliab would rally more men." Cuzbi held her stomach as if she was concerned not only for herself but for her baby.

Naomi resisted the urge to stand up for Eliab. *Comfort my friend, Lord.*

Hamul raised his sword and cackled as if he were half-mad. "We can raise more warriors."

Onan cast a sideways glance at his father-in-law. "We must act before dawn. Time is not our friend."

"And who is our friend?" Hamul continued. "Do we not serve the God of Abraham, Isaac, and Jacob? And did He not create man from mud?" Hamul sheathed his sword, slid from his mount, and rummaged in a saddlebag.

Cuzbi bent down and lifted Naomi's head covering from her ear. "Why is this man ranting about dirt while my husband's life is in danger? Is he mad?"

"His faith is strong," Naomi whispered.

"Father, we need to plan our defense of the city." Onan did not sound pleased with Hamul's interruption.

Hamul whirled around. He held a wooden mask aloft before donning it. Fanged teeth and oblong owl eyes replaced his normal features.

"We will craft an army of golems." The carved face muffled Hamul's declaration.

"Now I know he's mad," Cuzbi muttered.

"Maybe not."

Naomi left her friend and perched at Hamul's side. She took his mask and ran her fingers over the smooth cedar. The elders' heads swayed back and forth as if they agreed with Cuzbi's assessment of Hamul.

"I have heard stories of people coming to life from the mud. Did I believe them? I do not know if in my heart I did. But when I asked God to provide an army, He gave us four hundred men. Who am I to doubt that He could give us more warriors from the dust or from the heavens?"

"I have heard of golems." Eliab took the mask from her and placed it over his face. Removing it, he said, "A few survivors say when Gibeah was under siege, men dug in the dirt and made shapes out of clay. They prayed to God to breathe life into the forms and bring fighting men to protect the city. God did not create an army that day." He turned toward Onan. "I have buried the bodies of Benjamites who are now returning to dust. I do not want to bury any more people. Not this day. Let us make clay soldiers, but we must also plan our siege. We need to be in position before sunrise."

"Well then," Onan bellowed. He removed a beak-nosed mask from Hamul's satchel and strode closer to the lines of Judah's fighters. "I will need a few men to stay behind with the women and create an army of golems. And do not tell me that Israelites do not know how to make clay bricks."

Some older men came forward.

Onan gathered the elders and some division leaders into a group. Naomi listened while Cuzbi rattled on about her hardship in fleeing from the enemy.

"I will take two hundred men to the west," Onan said. "Our Benjamite brothers will lead almost as many east. With the outskirts burned, they will not leave scouts."

"I know these hills," Isa cut in. "I will show you

the best route before accompanying Eliab. May it not be said I abandoned the house of Berek."

"Leave the least men with me." Hamul rotated his gruesome mask. "I will hold the road. No army will venture down this path in fear that Judah has reinforcements from here to Jerusalem and on to Bethlehem. I can oversee the women now that it seems we will fight more than talk."

Was she staying? She cast a glance at Jael, who smothered Yom in her lap. Naomi wanted to be with Eliab and to speak for the girls of Shiloh. But what about her friends?

"At first light, I will blow the shofar three times." Onan's deep voice brought her back to their grim reality. "Then we will show them our strongholds. I will ride down to the gates of Gibeah, as will Eliab, and we will counsel with the commanders of Ephraim and Manasseh. This punishment of Benjamin will end by threat of war with Judah."

Agreement echoed through the circle.

War? Couldn't they avoid destruction?

While Onan divided the men, Naomi sought out Jael. Cuzbi remained atop her mount.

She stroked the young girl's arm. "We will be safe here with Hamul."

"I have been safe with you, Naomi. And I believe God will bring Isa back to me."

Naomi wished she could feel the surety that shone in Jael's eyes. She had lost two brothers in battle and had sat at her mother's side to comfort widows. Remembering the grief caused a millstone to settle in her stomach.

"We were going to carry your ewe, but we had to leave so fast." Jael clutched Yom so tight he bleated.

"The mother died in the flames. Forgive us."

Naomi's chest tightened. She cared about her gift, but not more than she cared for her friend's well-being. "There is nothing to forgive. You are here with me. How I would have grieved if you had perished."

"I will never return to Shiloh." Jael's lip quivered.

"You do not have to. We will rebuild our homes. What can fire do to rock?" She pinched Jael's chin. "But Isa will need the girl who fought off drunkards at his side, not a frightened sparrow."

An image of her mother, Heriah's proud wife, collapsing to the ground and rocking in the dirt after hearing of the deaths of cherished sons hollowed Naomi's stomach. She had tried to comfort her mother. For hours, over and over, she stroked her mother's back until her mother had enough strength to crawl through the doorway. *Don't swallow me up with such grief, Lord.* She flinched when Eliab's touch drew her into the shadows, away from her friends.

Tall, cloaked, and armed with a blade, Eliab transformed into a forbidding commander, but when she touched the bristle of his beard, all she could see were visions of him as a young shepherd caring for his family, and him caring for her.

Eliab held her against his body, disguising his bold embrace with the folds of his garment.

Sharing his warmth in such a daring, public display made her long for a wedding night.

"I am not leaving you behind like that Levite." Eliab's words rumbled deep in his chest. "I do not wish for you to face angry men. You are safest here, and I believe Hamul will keep you well, no matter what God wills. I would not go alone if—"

"You have to go. To save your family and mine.

God is with all the sons and daughters of Jacob, especially the weak." She stepped from the elixir of his warmth. "Go and save Gibeah."

"I am coming back for you, wife."

She glanced away from his consuming gaze, for she knew there was a chance he spoke a lie.

"You'd better, for you owe me a new loom and livestock."

"I owe you more than that. I owe you my life." He kissed her cheek and hesitated.

Was he waiting for her to be more brazen? A daring thought of taking hold of his hair and pushing against his breastplate flashed across her mind, but with her father and brother waiting not far to fight for her honor, and all the men milling about, she could not bring herself to be more bold. If all went as planned, she and Eliab would have a reunion later. And then? Her cheeks flamed hot.

"Go with God's protection," she said. "I will be right where I am, waiting for your return, husband."

In one swift movement, he cupped her face in his hands and kissed her like this could be their last. She held on to him and let him possess her mouth and take everything he needed, giving it with bountiful pleasure.

He broke their embrace.

She held on to her belly, still panting from their passion.

"I am coming back for you, Naomi. Very soon."

When Eliab left her sight, she thought her heart had come loose. Why had their meeting come with such chaos? Surely if things had been different, her father would have accepted an offer of marriage from such an upright man. She rested on God's promises that she would see Eliab again even though the clamor of war greeted her at every turn.

Onan and Eliab led the fighting men of Judah down the Camel Road with Isa at their side. The dirt quaked beneath her feet, but quiet ruled the hazy, dust-filled air. No one spoke of the potential battle ahead. The flatlands were a small journey away. Her temples pounded from thinking too much of evil. Was an ambush waiting in the hills? Were slingers camped in a crag? If only she could concentrate on the good.

She found Cuzbi and Jael near Hamul's mount, each holding a jeering mask.

Naomi shook her head.

"I'm surprised Hamul didn't give one to Yom."

Cuzbi peeked through the holes in the wooden face. "I believe that elder has been struck in the head one too many times and that is why he hands us these disguises."

Naomi checked to see if Hamul hovered nearby. "He rallied men to our cause. Be respectful, I beg."

"It was at Judah's urging that our husbands snatched us from the dance." Cuzbi set her mask on the ground. "Ashbanel confided as much."

Apparently, Ashbanel didn't realize that Hamul acted alone, and she was not going to tell tales on their protector. Not to a woman in the family way whose husband's life remained in peril.

She and Jael took turns corralling Yom. Chasing the lamb kept her mind free from worry. The animal must have sensed what they could not, for soon wind whipped through their camp.

Torch fires blew sideways. Hamul's horse high-stepped to avoid the flames. Naomi clutched her head covering tight around her face and retrieved rope from the supply cart to make a lead for Yom. Jael and Cuzbi looked like sacks of grain huddled together, covered head to toe with cloth.

"Where is that crazed elder?" The storm muffled Cuzbi's plea.

Naomi squinted down the road. Raindrops splashed on her nose. One. Then another. Then another. A shiver spiked from her toes to her tonsils. *Lord, do not send a flood.*

"In East Gibeah we had a roof," Cuzbi complained.

Jael peeked from her veil as the sky opened up and bathed the terrain with water.

Naomi stood in mud on a route bound for war. She might as well be swimming in the Jordan River for the soaking her clothes absorbed. How were Eliab and Isa weathering this downpour?

Lightning split the sky.

And for a brief second she saw Hamul. On the Camel Road. Scrambling her direction, mask in hand.

He called her name.

Hamul was disheveled when dry, but when wet, he was a possessed sight. His long hair looked like matted rabbit fur, and his jaw hung open as if he were drinking from the sky.

"God has sent us an army," he said as he pranced in the puddles.

Naomi scanned the dark horizon as best she could. She didn't see anything. No new movement. No new men.

"Where is this army?"

"Here." Hamul tapped the ground with his foot. "If God can make man from dirt, so can we."

Naomi glanced at the mud oozing into her

sandals. Perhaps Cuzbi had not misspoken about Hamul. Or perhaps she needed a stronger faith. Would she not do anything to save Eliab, her brother, or her father?

Scooping some mud from the path, she stared at the muck that Hamul believed would become an army.

"How do we bring them to life?"

24

Cuzbi dug in the mud with a shovel while Jael added bits of straw. Yom ate any donkey fodder the wind blew his direction. The rain had stopped, but Naomi took little consolation from the weather as she sank elbow deep in the muck of clay. Was it insanity to listen to Hamul? Or her last hope? For only God could breathe life into dirt. But she had to believe. She had to pray harder.

"I tell you that man is an idiot," Cuzbi said, her voice carrying like an out-of-tune lyre.

"Hush," Naomi scolded. "Hamul sent men to block the road. We don't want travelers wandering into our camp or into war."

"Camp? We are an outpost." Cuzbi rested her weight on the shovel and almost fell into their mud pit.

Naomi scooped a fistful of straw-studded clay from the ground and patted it into one of Hamul's masks. "We will be well defended if what Hamul says is true." She glanced at their elder as he secured fishing net from the supply cart to two torch poles. Giving the mud-filled mask to Jael, she said, "Go have Hamul inspect our first soldier."

Jael placed the sculpted mud on the nets for drying.

"I do not believe in golems." Cuzbi stabbed at the pit with her shovel. "God made Adam, not a bunch of weary women. And how many legions can we make by sunrise?"

Naomi pressed the stiff mud into another mask. "If the enemy believes these faces to be real, then this work is worth it, no matter the folly."

"A real army is preferable."

"Yes, but we don't have more soldiers. So we'll make them."

"Because you and Eliab did not amass enough fighting men."

"We did what we could." Mud splayed as Naomi beat clay into another mask. "The rest is up to God. Life, death, armies, war."

"Or whatever that foolish man has us do next."

Jael returned with an empty mask and bent down near the pit.

"I will help pack the faces. I do not mind tarrying in the dirt."

Cuzbi dug another mound of muck. "Vary the faces. Heaven help us if we have warriors that all look the same."

"That's the spirit." Jael grinned, her white teeth contrasting with her splattered cheeks.

Cuzbi flung a lump of clay in Jael's direction.

"Watch it, sister," Naomi said as she stood to balance another face on the nets. "That clump would make a perfect nose."

She chuckled and dodged another mud ball from Cuzbi.

When the sun hinted at its arrival, Hamul waddled over to the edge of their tomb-shaped pit.

"We must set our men onto the cliffs before our deed is visible. Have the girl carry the masks and you"—he pointed right at her finished sculpture—"have the mighty woman lift you up to place our spies."

Naomi halted her task. Her arms ached from pounding clay, but it was the hollowing pit in her stomach that filled her with unease. She wanted to be useful, but the last time she climbed on the side of a cliff was to rescue Eliab. If his life wasn't in danger, she never would have crawled to the edge and peered downward. She shivered at the remembrance and stilled. Wasn't his life in danger yet today?

"As you wish—"

"Oh, no." Cuzbi swung her shovel carelessly close to Hamul. "I am not climbing a hill. Not in my condition. My husband is an elder of Benjamin. Summon one of your soldiers."

Hands on hips, Hamul took a deep breath, pushed out his chest, and rose to his full height, which was half of Cuzbi's.

"My men are standing guard. How can I ask them to leave their posts?"

"I will place the golems on the hillside," Naomi offered. "Cuzbi will assist me." She held up a finger to her friend. "A man cannot touch my leg or waist. It appears you get the honor."

"I should have stayed in Gibeah." Cuzbi sighed in defeat.

"If you had, you'd be dead, or worse. Be thankful lifting my weight is your burden."

Jael handed her and Cuzbi a clay face. Cuzbi grumbled behind Naomi as she traipsed to where the Camel Road widened into a valley with Gibeah in the distance. Naomi surveyed the side of the hills as she followed a trail wide enough for a slim goat.

"We will position the faces where the land juts out. Our tribesmen will think reinforcements from Judah hide in the hills."

"What can mud and straw do for us? We are not priests or prophets. If your Hamul was truly a seer, wouldn't his son-in-law have taken him to fight instead of leaving him with the women?" Cuzbi picked at the dirt on her hand. "But for my husband's well-being, I will believe in the little man's schemes."

Naomi pressed the edges of her first soldier into the hillside. "That is all I ask, for I do not have a better plan. Hamul has fought in battle. I have only listened to stories."

Naomi noticed a cave below the apex of the cliff. "We should position a few men around that opening. Our enemies will fear slingers at such a height."

Cuzbi belly-laughed. "And how will they sling with no arms?"

"Where is your faith, sister? Give me a hand up." Naomi looped the satchel of golems over her shoulder.

"How about a push?" Cuzbi laced her fingers.

Naomi planted her sandal in Cuzbi's foothold and grasped a nearby rock. Pulling her weight upward, she wedged her other foot in a crevice and began an awkwardly slow ascent to the cave. Sunshine warmed her back and sent sweat dripping down her face. *Don't look down.* "Hear, O Israel." *Look above.* "The Lord is our God, the Lord alone." *A few more feet.* "I will love the Lord my God with all my heart." *Almost.* "With all my soul, and with all my might. And I pray this day that Your people, Lord, will counsel for peace." *There.*

She collapsed face first on a ridge, careful not to smash her soldiers.

With the rise of the sun, she had no time to slumber. She set two golems on the ground and hurried to the mouth of the cave to position a scout.

Pounding clay on stone, she made sure her soldier would not fall. She raced to retrieve another face, whirled around, and practically collided with a man.

Naomi dropped her mud soldier and clutched her pounding heart.

The silver-clad man, who had helped her with her mount, stepped closer. He was still a sight to behold, dressed for a fight fiercer than any Judahite she had seen, save Onan.

"I didn't know Hamul sent you to scout from up here? I thought you would be by Onan's side." Surely he had seen battle? Why did he stay behind, on a hill no less?

"I cannot see the arena from below."

"You are prepared for a siege." She knelt and tried to piece together the broken face, but her fingers trembled with the stranger so near. "We are hoping to prevent a war by sculpting an army out of mud."

The man stared far off into the distance.

What a fool he must think she was in crafting soldiers from dirt.

"Naomi, what is keeping you?" Cuzbi beckoned in hushed tones.

She peeked over the edge to assure Cuzbi of her safety, but one look at the drop sent her stomach swirling. She shut her eyes. The hollow sensation in her belly lessened.

"I am coming down." She kept her voice low. "There is a Judahite stationed in the cave." She turned toward the soldier. "It is of great comfort to know you are keeping watch over us."

A nod sent her on her way.

The long, humming howl of the shofar settled over her mud-caked flesh like a blanket. Onan blew the horn two more times. She rose and fixed her gaze to the east. A lone figure descended from the hills—Eliab upon his mount. He was but a speck of ink on a scroll.

Her chest sank as she scanned the divisions of fighting men from Ephraim and Manasseh. Rows of soldiers encircled the city, waiting to bring their justice to Gibeah. They covered the ground like parchment.

"Lord, we need a miracle. Send Your angels to protect my Eliab, his family, and mine."

She squinted westward to view Onan's descent, but no rider came forth.

She waited. She prayed the Shema. Not once. Several times. But only her Eliab galloped toward the masses.

25

Propelled as if by a rushing river, Naomi hurtled toward Cuzbi. Her friend made a gaped-mouth lunge to the side to prevent a collision. She did not have time for apologies with Eliab in peril. She had to find Hamul and convince him to ride out in Onan's stead.

"What is the hurry?" Cuzbi asked, steadying herself. "Has our ghost army awakened?"

Naomi reached for a jut to save a spill. "Onan did not show with his men."

"What do you mean? I heard the shofar."

"Yes, but he is nowhere in sight. Eliab is alone with only two hundred soldiers." Words rushed from her throat. "Hamul must represent Judah." She raced toward the Camel Road.

Cuzbi fell in step. "What if Onan has betrayed us?"

"I cannot believe it. I met his wife and family. Surely he would not be involved in such deceit."

Hamul remained near the cart with Jael.

"Elder," she shouted. "You must ride out and meet Eliab. My tribesmen will kill him. Your son-in-law tarries in the hills."

Mid-road, Hamul met her with his hands waving.

"You are mistaken. Onan came forth with this battle plan. He does not shy away from conflict."

"He is nowhere to be seen." She rested a hand on each of the elder's shoulders as her chest heaved. "Go to Eliab with your fighting men. Let the other tribes know Judah is here in force."

"Who will I bring? We are but a few stationed on the road."

Naomi's skin flushed as though she bathed in heated water. "You believe in golems, do you not? You saw a vision of a deliverer."

"Not of myself."

"Then who?"

The elder shrugged. "I do not know."

"Then send someone. Anyone. Dress them in your finery."

Hamul's brows furrowed. He took hold of her wrist.

She clutched the elder with the claws of a scavenger. Releasing her grip, she said, "I beg of you. Ride out for Judah and Benjamin."

The elder shook his head. "I cannot leave this place. What of these women in my care? Take one of my men. He will tell the others you speak on my behalf and for the elders of Judah. Sereb is not here to protest."

"Who will listen to me? I am a grape picker's daughter," Naomi said.

"Go. Find a soldier." Tears muddied Cuzbi's cheeks. "You started this journey with Eliab. Now finish it for all of us."

Jael tugged on Naomi's tunic. "I will go with you."

"No." Naomi softened her short response with an embrace. "Stay with Cuzbi," she whispered. "She will need someone to care for her if Ashbanel falls."

Jael shivered like a caged bird.

Naomi rubbed the girl's mud-caked back. "Do not fear for Isa. I know of no one who could get near him if he has rocks to sling."

Jael's eyes widened. "You sound as if you are not coming back?"

"I wish I knew what God has planned. I do not know the future, but I know who should accompany me." She kissed Jael one last time and trotted backward toward the golem-laden cliff. "Find me a cloak. I will not impress anyone covered in clay." Removing her faded indigo head covering, she called out, "Bring me some linen for another veil. This rag will not do." She rolled up the soiled cloth and sent it sailing toward the cart. "To think that former sash was supposed to catch me a husband."

"Do not be so hasty." Cuzbi bent to pick up the rag. "It caught us all husbands."

Naomi snorted out a weak laugh and then scaled rock, mud, and crushed stone like a mountain goat. Scanning the valley, hoping for a sign of Onan, her wish went unfulfilled. Eliab was nowhere in sight. Rows of soldiers had swallowed him up.

Huffing until her lungs burned, she called out for the scout. When she reached the landing, he stepped from the cave.

"I am in need of a companion." She braced her hands on her knees as bursts of light clouded her vision. "Onan and his men have not come down from the hills. My husband is riding into a massacre. If we travel out and speak for Hamul, we might prevent another blood bath."

"Why should the protection of Benjamin be my concern?"

Naomi gasped. "If it is not, why are you here? To watch the descendants of Jacob kill one another?"

The man did not move. He stood and surveyed the

encampments as if he watched a Passover procession.

"Stay if you will. I did not realize cowards were born in Bethlehem." Her temples pulsed with each syllable spoken. She turned to leave. "I will find another escort."

"Naomi *bat* Heriah."

How dare he address her using her given name? He had disregarded her petition to save Eliab. She faced the traitor.

"I have nothing more to say to you." Her voice warbled like a rooster.

"That is a shame, daughter of Heriah, for the Most High God has heard your prayers."

"What are you saying? You do not know what I speak to God."

"You did pray for an angel, did you not?" He crossed his leather-clad arms.

"I believe I prayed for a legion of angels. Enough to prevent a war."

The soldier did not look pleased with her brazen answer. "Am I not enough for you?"

Who or what was this spy claiming to be? Surely he was not God's messenger? He had taken orders from Onan and brought her a mule. Was he kin to Hamul? She tried to answer his question but no words traveled to her tongue.

"Fear not." The scout stepped into the darkness of the cave. His body glowed as if he were made of nothing more than a fiery vapor. The brightness burned her eyes.

Sinking to her knees, she bowed with her face to the ground. "Forgive my anger. I misspoke when I believed you to be the enemy. I should not have questioned your stature."

"You did not speak falsely. You fear for Eliab."

She nodded with a head as heavy as a stocked wagon. "I am in love with Eliab. In the beginning, I did not know Eliab's heart. I thought all the Benjamites unlawful. But that is not true. Eliab follows God's ways. He is a good man who does not deserve to be murdered. Nor do his people. No one does."

"Then you must go to him." The messenger returned to the daylight, but his presence held an impressive aura she had not noticed beforehand.

"How can I bring justice without an army or an elder? Yarn and vines I understand. I have never been in battle or spoken to an assembly of warriors. You must go with me."

"Do you trust God to act on Benjamin's behalf?"

Did she? After all the suffering that had befallen Eliab's people?

"Yes." Her affirmation wavered.

"Then you alone must talk with the elders of Ephraim and Manasseh, for your eyes have been opened to the truth."

"Alone?" Surely God's messenger could do this better.

"I could."

Her mouth fell open. He knew her thoughts.

"You, daughter of Heriah, have a heritage in Ephraim, and now you have a family in Benjamin. Speak to your father and the elders from Shiloh. Show them the forgiveness that reigns in your heart. Share your hope for a future. Tell them what you have told me."

Pressure pulsed behind her eyes. She knew the stubbornness of her father and of her people. And by the messenger's anchored stance, he did not seem swayed to accompany her.

"What if I have need of you?" She cleared the emotion from her throat. "How do I summon your help?"

The angel came and bent down, bathing her in shade. "With a prayer. Just like you have always done. The Most High will answer." He rose and touched a hand to his hip. "When you are most afraid, listen for the shofar."

"The horn is of little comfort when no one heeds its call." She blinked under his assessment. "My lord."

"This time, I will blow it and God will act."

"Praise be to the God of Abraham, Isaac, and Jacob." She backed away in a crawl, feeling with her foot until she reached the edge.

"Toda raba," she said before racing down the landscape and knocking a few golems to an early death.

When her feet hit the road, she sprinted toward Cuzbi, who held out a hooded cloak the color of aged wine.

Cuzbi opened the sleeve. "Sister, you are trembling."

"I almost fell. What a silly fright I have. Do not worry. I can still ride." Her words stumbled upon each other. Did she even make sense?

Jael handed her a dyed-mustard belt.

"Where is your escort?" Hamul asked. "My mount is ready, as is your donkey."

Fluttering her hand toward the road, she said, "He is waiting up ahead." Not a total lie. The messenger did sit upon the cliff.

With a boost from Jael, she perched on Hamul's horse and took command of the reins.

Hamul's face crinkled like a raisin. "How is the man known? I do not remember who is spying from the cliff."

"I do not know his name. We will thank him later."

She kicked Hamul's horse into a gallop.

"Where is the other?" Hamul bellowed.

She did not look back, but she slowed her mount when she reached the flatlands, not wanting the soldiers to think her a threat. Without a helmet, a slinger's stone could crush her skull.

Someone had to ride out and speak some sense into this wild assembly. Unfortunately, she did not think it would be her, unaccompanied, with no fighting men in her wake. But she had the assurance of God's messenger.

Do what is right and good in the Lord's sight, so that it may go well with you.

She repeated the scripture over and over. She did not need to take over the Promised Land—she just needed to ask her tribesmen to return home without their daughters and without a bride price.

Do it. For Eliab, Cuzbi, and Jael.

A wafting scent of sweat-drenched bodies baked by the sun sent her stomach into spasms. She swaddled her cloak about her face and veered nearer to where she had seen Eliab enter the lines of men. Hamul's mount pranced onward as if he knew he belonged at the front of the field.

As she neared the camps, a path formed for her to pass. She pulled on the reins, keeping her mount a few yards from the gathering. She was aware that the access they granted could close in around her, leaving her defenseless.

I can do this.

Breathing through her mouth, she ignored the stench wafting to her nostrils. She dug deep for a commanding voice that would carry beyond the first few rows of fighters. Sitting tall, she cleared her throat, removed the hood of her cloak, and raised her right arm.

"I come in the name of Hamul, elder of Judah, seeker of peace. Judah stands with Benjamin. Hamul requests a meeting of the tribal elders to put an end to this siege."

"'Tis a woman," someone shouted.

Murmurs rippled through the crowd.

"Where are your leaders?" she called. "What of the elder who came before me?"

A bare-chested man approached. He wore no robe as a sign of honor, but his body spoke of the readiness to fight, for the muscles he displayed could only come from the rigor of training. He held a long spear. This was no walking stick.

"Where is Judah?" the fighter chastised. "The Benjamite deceives about his strength in number. Am I to pay heed to a Judahite's concubine? Where is Hamul?"

Who was this man to hurl insults? She clenched the leather reins.

"My elder waits on the road with divisions of men." She made it sound as if warriors from all of Judah's cities readied to charge out. "You have seen a portion of his men from the east." She flipped her hand like a queen dismissing a servant.

"Hah. What do we care about a few hill dwellers? We joined with Ephraim to bring justice to this wrongdoing."

How could this man boast in the face of annihilation? Had the tribes not seen enough death from their battles with Benjamin? Did he want more bloodshed? Hardheaded fool.

"There are more Judahites on the road and in the hills. Many more." Her voice faltered like her assurance.

Her war-scarred adversary laughed. Others joined in.

Scrambling to her knees for height, she trusted Hamul's horse to hold steady.

"Why would I lie when Ephraim is in danger? I am the daughter of Heriah, an Ephraimite, taken from the feast." Her heart rallied against the fists she held to her breast. "Shall I let Judah spill my people's blood? I have lost two brothers to war and I will not lose another. We have suffered enough. Let the elders settle this matter. That is all I ask."

"Then let Judah's elders show themselves." He motioned toward some men. "Any captive that speaks for Judah speaks for Benjamin and is a traitor to me and my legions."

A mob of men approached her mount.

She refused to be dragged down in a crowd of angry warriors from Manasseh. God was with her.

What had Eliab instructed when they were attacked by the Moabites? Stay upright. Kick. Use the reins as a whip. Oh, how she wished he was sitting behind her. His parting at sunrise seemed like days.

A soldier reached for her ankle.

Furious, she snapped the reins back and forth as though she were harvesting wheat. Leather grazed the horse's withers. He reared in displeasure. Grabbing hold of the mane left her distracted and undefended.

A man plucked her from her perch, but he did not catch her fall. Her spine struck the ground. Air rushed from her lungs. She elbowed and kicked anyone who dared to grab her cloak, willing to share the pain that radiated across her back. Hands clawed at her limbs like dogs on raw meat.

"Stop at once."

Father? She welcomed the familiar voice of reason.

"I am Heriah, and that girl is my daughter."

Her father stood above her with Nadab, her brother, at his side.

Scrambling into his arms, she held him fast, breathing in the memories of home, of vineyards, sour wine, and security. She had prayed for this moment and it had come to pass. She no longer clung to him for escape, but for reason. She pulled from his embrace.

"Father, please listen to me. Judah waits in the hills. They request a council of elders." Taking hold of her brother's hand, she kissed it. "We cannot lose another. You are father's only heir."

Nadab drew back. "You are filthy. What have they done to you to make you speak such drivel?"

"We must stop a war." Had he not seen enough death? Spinning around, she beseeched the crowd. "How can we love the Lord and kill our own people? What is the harm in a council? Can we not talk among ourselves?" At the peak of her vocal range, she called for the elders of Ephraim.

Nadab tried to shush her summons. "She has been tortured by the Benjamites. My sister is mad." He grabbed hold of her arm. "Look for yourselves at this sorcery."

She slipped from her cloak and stood in her clay-stained robe. "I am not possessed. Seek out Judah's leaders. It is all I ask."

Zicri *ben* Ithamar, an elder of her tribe, stepped from behind the gawking soldiers.

Thank You, Lord.

"What is this outburst? First, we have the Benjamite, and now one of our own?"

Naomi bowed low. "Elder, the leaders of Judah request a meeting to hear your grievances and to restore unity among our tribes."

The spear-toting warrior strode toward her with the crazed eyes of a killer.

"This is a distraction, a ploy by Benjamin to gain time. Judah has not shown themselves. And they are not known to be cowards. Why would they hide behind this whore?"

"Silence yourself. She is my daughter," Heriah shouted.

"And what is she worth when she is groveling for the men who defiled her?"

"Enough," Zicri said. He consulted robed men Naomi did not recognize. Were they elders of Manasseh? These same unarmed men dispersed through the crowd.

Zicri came and stood before her.

She bowed, knees trembling, and stared, blinking into the elder's bearded face.

"You speak for Judah now, do you? How did our brothers to the south know we camped around the city?"

Her body became as light as a bed sheet blowing in the wind, but she did not look away from the elder she had known since birth. She had gone to Judah, not as a traitor to her people, but as a daughter, and as a sister, and as a woman wanting to end the bloodshed, not to bring it forth.

"I went—"

"See." The warrior readied his spear. "She brought an army against us."

Her father stepped forward, sword drawn.

Zicri demanded the soldier lower his weapon. "Let us hear the girl."

"I went to spare my father the loss of another son." Her throat tightened as grief overwhelmed her conscience. "I went because I saw a goodness in the men of Benjamin. I saw a respect for the Law and our prophets and I did not want them to be wiped from this land. How can the sons of Joseph slay the sons of his only brother, Benjamin? How?" The force of her question burned her throat. Her tongue tasted like salty bile.

"Her alliance is not with Ephraim or Manasseh," the spearman jeered.

"She has been mistreated." Her father stationed himself at her side.

Her father's defense buoyed her strength. She rose and leaned into his side for support.

The robed elders of Manasseh jostled through the onlookers and returned to the small arena formed by Zicri, his kin, and her family. One of the elders pushed Eliab forward.

Eliab was alive. *Selah.* Her shoulders sagged with relief, but her spirit soared.

Standing defiant with a swollen eye and torn robe, the son of Berek cast a glance at every man that mattered. He fixed her with a look that begged her to stay safe.

Every muscle in her arms tightened. An ache ricocheted through her heart. How could they mistreat a leader of a tribe? One who came in the name of Judah and Benjamin?

Zicri marched her toward Eliab. "Did this man take you to Judah to speak on Benjamin's behalf?"

The assembly hushed.

Eliab's gaze held no fear. His brown eyes possessed a quiet strength. She glanced toward Gibeah. Did Berek know his son was dangerously close to being sacrificed for trying to save the city? How many Benjamites and their wives waited in terror for their fate to be known? She scanned the far-off hills. Was there an army to come to her rescue? An angel army? An army of golems?

"Are you deaf? Answer my question." Zicri shook her shoulder.

Eliab flinched. "Speak the truth, Naomi."

A rush of heat flamed across her skin. Her father stood so tall, so proud. She raised her eyes to the heavens and squinted at the thick rays of light shining around the city as if no clouds blocked the sun. A warm fullness overcame her soul. *Do what is right and good in the Lord's sight, so that it may go well with you.*

Back straight, brushing off dust from her sleeve, she readied to speak the truth. "This man did not take me to Judah. I asked to accompany him. I went to speak on behalf of the daughters of Shiloh who wish to remain with their Benjamite husbands."

A loud roar filled her ears as her father tore his tunic.

Her brother advanced with knife drawn. "You desire a Benjamite?"

Not wanting to become a widow before she became a wife, she slipped her father's blade from his belt, evaded her brother's grasp, and lunged into

Eliab's waiting arms.

Then, and only then, did a mighty shofar blast resound from the hill to the heavens.

26

The sound of the shofar filled the camps of fighting men with a haunting howl. Naomi's hand trembled as she held her father's blade in front of her and Eliab. Her palms were as slick as stones submerged along the Jordan. She slashed the sword back and forth lest someone slap it from her hand. Eliab's arm grew taut around her waist.

What sort of army was the messenger bringing into the valley? God's army? An angel army? Or an army of mud men?

Warriors readied their weapons. The men of Ephraim and Manasseh scrambled into position. Battle lines formed. Bur her father stood idle and unarmed. His face was drawn like he had worked a full day in the fields.

She choked back the emotion damming her throat and concentrated on saving her people from a slaughter. All of her people. Benjamites, Ephraimites, and all the descendants of Jacob.

Zicri edged closer to Eliab, staying out of reach of the sway of her sword tip. "Sheath that blade and speak of Judah's plans. What do you know of this siege?"

"Now you believe our petition?" Eliab held her arm steady, but he did not lower their weapon. "Did we not warn of Judah's assembly and ask that a council be held?"

A young soldier ran toward Zicri. "Leader," he gasped. "Divisions of men are coming from the east, west, and even more from the south."

Finally, Onan had shown himself. But who did Hamul bring? Had the messenger of God breathed life into the golems?

Calling for his mount, Zicri turned to address her husband. "You two will come with me and my fellow elders."

"Not without the animals we rode into camp." Eliab did not budge, but he lowered their sword. "I am an elder from the tribe of Benjamin. My position and my people deserve your respect, as does my wife."

Eliab placed his hand on her shoulder, and as much as she wanted to take comfort in his show of affection, she could not grasp his hand in front of her father.

Zicri pointed at Nadab. "Find their horses. Has your sister not brought me enough trouble? She rallied Judah to defend her lover."

Naomi's cheeks grew hot. Had she not tried to save Ephraim from bloodshed?

Sliding his hand down her back, Eliab gave her a slight push toward her father. Even though Eliab escorted her, her feet barely moved, as if they were sunken in Hamul's mud pit. Would her father retaliate against Eliab? Against her? He had no weapon at the moment, but he could call on family for revenge.

She could barely meet her father's scowl. They had become like foreigners to each other.

Eliab stood broad-shouldered at her side. "I cannot ask for your daughter's hand, Heriah, nor can you give her to me." His voice cracked as if he were a suitor capable of being cast off. "I never meant to cause your household harm. I sought a way around an oath, for a way to have an heir." Eliab held out Heriah's sword. "This belongs to you. I am not a thief."

Her heart cinched so tight she thought it would burst. "Forgive us, Father."

Her brother, flanked by two harvesters from Shiloh, emerged from the mass of fighting men with two mounts for her and Eliab.

"Come along," Zicri snapped. "We need to lead the men."

Zicri, the leader she had known since birth, barked commands from his lips instead of the soothing words of wisdom she remembered. Her muscles tensed. Was she not the same girl he counseled in Shiloh?

Eliab took hold of her hand. "My wife will ride with me. Give Hamul's mount to Heriah."

Gratitude flowed from her heart, down her arm, and into the squeeze she gave her husband's grasp.

With a click of his tongue, Zicri said, "He is a laborer. I have witnessed his family's field work for years."

"He is my father-in-law." Eliab ignored the elder's protest and mounted his horse. She took her place behind him.

Heriah hesitated to sit atop a horse emblazoned with Judah's emblems.

"Join us, Father. Is it not your right to hear the reasoning behind the raid?"

Her father nodded. "I will ride at an elder's request." He mounted without a glance toward his tribal elder—Zicri—or his son.

Nadab strode away, armed and ready for a fight. She had gone to Judah to prevent deaths, especially within her own family, and if it took every last breath, she would keep Nadab and her father safe.

She, Eliab, and her father rode with Zicri to where the other elders of Ephraim and Manasseh waited. They passed lines of men, row after row, who threw in their lot with the tribal leaders.

Naomi squinted at the flatlands surrounding Gibeah, into what was once again a desert battleground. She had never seen fighting men facing off for war. Her soul shivered to think this is what her brothers beheld before they died. She shook the vision from her head. God was among them and He was a just God.

Finally, Onan had arrived to aid Isa's divisions. The city was flanked from the east to the west by men from the tribes of Ephraim and Manasseh, but their armies were a small sparrow compared to the mass of men flowing from the Camel Road and fanning out in front of the cliffs. Two new riders led the impressive show of strength.

"You emptied the cities and the whole countryside against us," Zicri said, his voice hushed for only the leaders to hear.

Eliab's back arched at the sight of his defenders. "I do not have that kind of influence in Bethlehem."

"We know one that does," she whispered.

Her pulse raced as Judah's horsemen approached. Not a one was God's messenger. Where was he? As the riders neared, she grasped Eliab's robe as if she were dangling from a cliff. The sight of the dark, bearded man in a turban coiled her stomach. The last time she had seen Sereb, he had stormed from Onan and Abigail's home. Amram would not ride to Gibeah. Had these men decided to fight against Benjamin? Surround their own elders with warriors? "What is Sereb doing here? And Amram?"

Before Eliab could answer, Hamul popped his head from behind Sereb's flowing robe.

"They would not bring Hamul if they meant us harm," Eliab said.

She thanked God for that half-crazed man.

Judah's elders halted a short distance away.

Onan's horse pranced forward. The commander stretched his leather-banded arms wide and shouted, "Glad to have you, brothers." Onan's cocked head and wide-eyed stare made it seem that he too did not expect Sereb's arrival.

"Why does Judah concern itself in Ephraim's matters?" Zicri called across the clearing. "Do we not have authority when it comes to our people?"

"It concerns all of our people," Onan shouted. He addressed all the fighting men as if they were his own. "We took an oath in haste. We let the blood of our kin taint our thoughts. Vengeance ruled and not wisdom."

"Who has bewitched you?" Zicri asked. "You desire mercy for the wicked?"

"Yahweh has spoken." Onan's retort resounded over the armies.

Hearing the Lord's name reminded Naomi that they were not alone.

Onan rode closer until he was within striking distance of a sword.

Mutterings fell silent.

"My men and I waited in the hills to show ourselves. I sounded the shofar. My fellow elder, Eliab, came from the east with his men." Onan indicated Isa and his divisions with a sweep of his arm. "My men and I were struck blind by a light so bright it could only come from our God. We could not see until the last ram's horn wailed."

Manasseh's leaders chuckled. "The sun blinded you and we are to be convinced it was God?" the eldest asked. "Rain pelted us. Perhaps you were struck by lightning?"

"You scoff?" Onan's tone rose with disbelief. "Am I not an elder and a seasoned warrior? Would a flash of light render me useless?"

Sereb trotted his horse so it was nose to nose with Zicri's mount. Hamul slid down and stood, arms crossed, face scowling, as if these elders were children needing a scolding.

"I cannot speak to Onan's ordeal," Sereb began. "I, for one, did not want to fight for Benjamin. But since the Sabbath ended, I have had no rest. I have heard the constant crying of a woman." Sereb cast a glance at her. "This daughter from Shiloh challenged me to come and fight for the descendants of Jacob's youngest son. She told me how Rachel would weep for her children."

Rachel's grief. A strange hum rang in Naomi's ears. Did she believe her own words?

Zicri balked. "You ride against us because of someone's trickery?"

"Because of that girl." Sereb pointed her direction.

Hiding behind Eliab tempted her, but instead, she peered over Eliab's shoulder and skimmed over everyone's stare.

"As sure as I sit here, I heard the cries of Jacob's wife and Benjamin's mother." Sereb's face showed no humor. "Rachel had but two sons: the tribe of which you stand to destroy, and Joseph, the forefather of your tribes. God used the constant cries to beckon me to gather an army and follow the other leaders of Judah. My ears fell silent at the last horn blast. Is it by chance my ears quieted when Onan's sight was restored?"

Zicri began shaking his head before Sereb had finished speaking. "Nonsense. Are we to believe this girl is a prophetess? The tribe of Benjamin has broken God's Law. Why would God come to their defense?"

"You left us no choice but to break God's Law." Eliab matched Zicri's arrogant elder-speak. "We stole because we had no women. No children. No future."

Bickering began among the elders. Hamul strode into the huddle of leaders and whistled loud and long.

"Eliab does not lie." Hamul grasped Eliab's arm and patted him on the lower back.

At this moment, she would take any affirmation of her husband from an elder of Judah.

Hamul paced around the tribunal. "We left a tribe of Israel with no hope of survival. To beget heirs, they would have to marry foreign women. Is that not breaking God's command?" Hamul shrugged and threw up his hands as if in worship. "Whether from a godly vision, or from my own absurdity, I am not sure, but I told Berek about the feast in Shiloh. I have known Ephraimites and Judahites who have married dancers and married well."

"And what of the fathers?" someone yelled. Naomi knew her father's voice. "Did you not think of their grief?"

She fought the tears pressing to be released. She had to stay strong for Eliab. For herself.

"What grief is that?" Onan asked. "That you had one less woman to feed or that no coin or livestock changed hands?"

"How dare you insult us?" Zicri's face reddened.

"Let us call on Berek, the leader of Benjamin. He can tell us of his intent." Onan positioned a hand near his sword. "We can kill each other's sons or we can listen to an elder's reason."

Hamul walked toward his decorated mount. "I will summon Berek." He reclaimed his horse from her father while angry voices rose among the ranks.

"Lord, show Yourself. Stop these insults," she prayed.

"Rise! Silence this discord. I will speak the truth through you." The answer roared in her ear.

27

The elders continued to quarrel. Each leader shook a fist or pounded his chest as he shouted over the others, spitting accusations. Naomi knelt on Eliab's mount and then stood. Placing a hand on each of Eliab's shoulders, she willed her knees not to buckle. Eliab turned his head and regarded her with a confident smile as if he had been waiting for her boldness.

"Berek's testimony should be heard." She did not shout, but she took the tone of a ruler.

A few elders scoffed at her interruption.

"My father-in-law's reasoning will not change my intention. I have found a God-fearing Benjamite, who I have chosen to be my husband."

Rumblings continued among the circle of men.

"If I am willing to forgive my captor and start a life in this barren land, then shouldn't the elders who taught me to forgive allow their brothers to rebuild this tribe? Even with their own daughters?"

"Who is this woman to lecture us?" a leader of Manasseh retorted.

"She speaks not only by my authority," Eliab said, "but she speaks on her own accord. Does she not know firsthand about the abduction?"

Sereb clapped his hands. His decorated Judahite armor glimmered in the sun. "If she can challenge me in my house, she can challenge all of us in this council."

Naomi's skin heated like a refiner's furnace as all elders observed her with renewed interest. "I not only seek what is best for myself, but I seek what is best for my fellow sisters. Many women wish to remain and rebuild this tribe. Do we not teach that we are one people, with one purpose? Will God not be served if I bear a child to worship Him in a land that once perverted His teaching?"

A loud whinny caused the leaders to turn away before anyone answered her challenge to let the women stay. Troops stepped apart, forming a path so the large animal and its riders could pass. Berek rode in on Hamul's mount, with Hamul settled on the rump of the horse. Curious whispers buzzed in the Benjamite leader's wake.

Berek acknowledged Eliab. Her father-in-law met the gaze of every elder. "I do not believe I could have said it better." His calm yet commanding praise silenced the council.

"You must say something about the raid on my feast." Zicri seemed none too pleased with her defense of the abductions.

Berek surveyed the leaders as well as the soldiers standing nearby. "I know what it is to lose a daughter. I lost two in the slaughter at Gibeah." His voice faltered. "I also lost my wife and a son. I have seen my tribe cut down to six hundred men. What hope for a future did we have with no wives and no children?"

Hamul stretched his neck to be seen over Berek's shoulder. "I meant no harm in sharing my thoughts on the festival. I gave comfort to Berek and myself."

"With our daughters," Zicri reminded the crowd.

Naomi bristled at her elder's reprimand. "Those

daughters are now wives and some are already with child." The pressure in her chest threatened to burst her bones. "You did not break an oath, and I have formed a bond here in Benjamin. Do not force me to break it. For I will not."

Her father elbowed his way into the circle of elders. "So you fled to Judah to force us to leave?"

Eliab placed a hand over hers. She longed for the turmoil to end. She longed to be his wife in every way. She longed for it sooner, rather than later.

"No, Father. I went to Bethlehem to keep my family from bloodshed. To save your lives." She pressed her lips together, but they quivered all the more.

Berek twisted to face Zicri. "I sent my sons into your vineyards so my tribe would survive. And what of you, Ephraim?" He beheld Sereb. "And you, Judah?" He turned and faced the leaders of Manasseh. "And what of you, descendants of Joseph? Would you not do the same?"

Contemplative quiet fell upon the council. Elders talked, but in hushed tones.

She settled behind Eliab, encircling his waist with her arms. She did not need to steady her body, but his warmth helped to calm her nerves. *Have I said enough, Lord?* Berek was here to speak for his tribe.

Zicri's mount angled forward. "Ephraim will not condemn our brothers if it means a war with Judah."

"Neither will Manasseh fight." A burly elder spoke for the group. He turned toward them. "Are we not all Rachel's children? I do not sense a lawlessness in our brothers."

Thank You, Lord.

Berek cleared his throat as tears streamed down

his cheeks. "If there are women who wish to return, I will not stop them. I have not heard of such. Perhaps, when a man knows he has been blessed with a special gift, he loves with a heart of gratitude."

"Yes, yes." Hamul bobbed up and down. "That is why God spoke through me."

"Father," Onan said quickly. "You are not God's mouthpiece."

"I know He speaks through others." Hamul gave her a knowing wink.

Had he seen the messenger on the cliff?

Hamul motioned toward some men amassed behind Sereb. A few faces resembled the fang-toothed masks Hamul had distributed. Golems? Or coincidence?

"Toda raba," she mouthed to her small, scheming elder.

"The Lord has brought us to peace this day." Berek's voice rose over the crowd. "Let us sup together as one people. May you find hospitality in Gibeah once again."

"Hear, O Israel," Eliab began. "The Lord is our God. The Lord alone."

Her spirit rejoiced as everyone joined in. "Love the Lord your God with all your heart, with all your soul, and with all your might."

Her father came and stood a few feet from Eliab's mount. His expression remained stoic. "Love your neighbor as yourself." He recited the phrase as if trying to convince himself to believe it, and then he drew closer. "Let it not be said the house of Heriah seeks vengeance."

She slid from her horse and went to her father. She did not hug him as a young daughter would do, but with every ounce of strength she possessed, she held back and wrung her hands, willing herself to address him as a married woman. "I am a proud daughter. You raised me in wisdom and truth." She could not stop a tear from cascading down her cheek. "I worry for Nadab. His heart is still hard."

Her father's brow furrowed, reminding her of all the rows her family dug together in the fields. "It will soften in time."

She tried to smile, but her lips would not curve upward, and her tears would not stay hidden. Salty drops seeped into the gaps made by her mouth. "I believe hearts will soften. Someday."

Eyes closed, Heriah bestowed upon her a half-nod.

Eliab came and faced her father. "There is not enough gold in Benjamin to pay you for what your daughter is worth to me. It would have been my honor to arrange a betrothal with you." Bending at the waist, Eliab showed his respect. "When my land and my flocks are fruitful, I will remember you."

"Elder." Her father cleared his throat. "Your wife is a skilled weaver."

A wellspring burst forth in her soul at her father's praise.

"She will have a loom again, for the one I provided was lost in a fire."

Naomi grasped her father's hand. It was dry and calloused just as it had always been. "I will make you a robe of scarlet and indigo so everyone will take notice. Mother's will be of many colors."

"I cannot return to Gibeah." Her father's reply came out faint, but with a finality. "And you will have a family to tend to here."

She struggled to breathe. An enormous ache

overtook her chest as if it had been cinched with rope.

"But if you send a robe, I will wear it for all of Shiloh to see." Her father's gaze met hers.

For a moment she was his little girl, but only for that moment, for her heart told her otherwise. "Then I will send it." Another rebel tear slid down her face.

With an acknowledgement of Eliab, Heriah turned and withdrew among his tribesmen.

She strained to watch her father's retreat. She had seen this man almost every day of her life, and now she did not know if or when she would see him again. The dam of tears, waiting to be released, pulsed behind her eyes and behind her temples.

Eliab drew her into his chest and swept the wetness from her cheeks. "Come, after I am done here, let us go toward East Gibeah and see our home and what I need to rebuild."

"Our home." Holding his hands against her face, she said, "Let us see what we need to rebuild. Together."

28

"We should be heading south, not east," Naomi said as she and Eliab rode toward what remained of their home. This time, she sat in front of Eliab, facing forward, his arms strong and tight around her waist. The night of the raid, she had despised the man she now called her husband. This day, she desired to show him her love.

Eliab rested his chin on her head. "I saw Isa heading to the Camel Road. He will not leave Jael alone."

"And Cuzbi?"

"From what I have seen of my sister-in-law, she has most definitely stormed the city and complained to Ashbanel about her hardship."

Naomi grinned. "How perceptive of you, my husband."

Pulling their mount to a halt a short distance from the house of Berek, Eliab jumped from his horse. He helped her dismount and then traipsed toward the main building.

"The roof is gone and the rock is charred. I have rebuilt worse rubble."

Even in the solitude, a pounding rhythm echoed through her skull. She hated the aftermath of war. She and Eliab had both seen death, but he was the only one to have seen destruction. Now it was her turn to view the shattered pottery and the possessions reduced to ash.

"Wherever you lay your head is my dwelling," she said.

He pressed a kiss to her forehead. "We shall lie together soon."

The clop, clop, clop of hooves interrupted their embrace.

Her head snapped up.

The messenger approached on a horse as white as a polished pearl.

Naomi dropped to her knees. She urged Eliab to do the same. "He is from the heavens," she whispered.

She bowed her head. "Lord, You answered my prayers and spared my family."

"I am not the Lord, but one who does His bidding. Did you not do what I asked of you? You spoke your truth to the elders?"

She nodded, her throat as dry as desert dust. "Thanks be to God."

The messenger dismounted and strode toward the two-story structure where she and Eliab slept. His armor glistened like chiseled gems. She blinked at the glittering display.

"Eliab *ben* Berek, your home is in need of repair. Is there not a shepherd's pit nearby?"

"Not far," Eliab said.

"And this is your wife?" The messenger fixed his gaze upon Eliab.

"We have had a betrothal period. Yes." Eliab's voice faltered.

"In Bethlehem, you both declared yourselves for each other in front of witnesses. Now, take your wife into the cave. Shield yourselves and wait for my call."

Eliab grabbed her hand. For once, he shook and

she did not.

They raced toward the sunken pit, the thud of their sandals filling the air.

As they entered the shadowy darkness of the cave, Eliab asked, "How are you known to him?"

Struggling to catch her breath, she placed a hand to her parched throat. "I saw him upon the cliff before you rode out to meet Onan. I thought he was a scout." How did she describe his beauty?

"Until?"

"He stepped into a cave like this one and became like the sunrise. Bright. Beautiful. A sight to behold."

"You did not speak of it?" Eliab seemed surprised and yet a rumble of disappointment kept his voice even.

She sighed and took his hands. "Would you have believed me? Or would you have thought I was Hamul's daughter with a silly story?"

Somehow he managed to escape her hold. He pulled her close. "Yes." His mouth brushed the side of her face. "And yes." His breath bathed her lips.

The ground beneath her feet began to quake as if cattle stampeded nearby. She grabbed onto Eliab as the earth rocked like waves on the open sea. She dropped to her knees. Pebbles cascaded from crevices in the rock above. Eliab covered her with his body.

"We will be safe," she said, her words muffled by the folds of her skirt. She attempted to say more, but a howl whipped through the dark area, accompanied by a wild wind.

Eliab's grip tightened around her waist. "Do not fear. God is with us."

God was with them. A few feet away. She began to chuckle at the thought of how her journey had ended.

Eliab must have thought her scared, for he caressed her arm. She turned her head to speak, but dust clouded the cave, and she began to cough.

The threat of the storm waned while the ground stilled its shaking. She and Eliab stood. His protective grasp still lingered on her skin.

"Son of Berek?" The summons echoed in the enclosed space.

Eliab jumped backward and steadied himself with a hand upon the wall. She straightened and wrapped her arms about her body, willing her nerves to withstand a few more hours of daylight.

"Come forth." The messenger's voice was loud but kind.

Scrambling out of the cave, they climbed the stone steps of the pit as if in a race. Naomi halted, slack-jawed. Her husband stopped at her side.

"He performed a miracle." Naomi scanned the thatched roofs, the unblemished stones, the clean walls, and the clay jars lining the cooking courtyard.

"Praise be to God," Eliab shouted, slumping to his knees.

The messenger mounted his porcelain-hued horse.

She ran to catch him. "I do not know how to thank you."

Casting a glance at Eliab before fixing his fiery-eyed stare upon her, he said, "This place is too quiet. Be fruitful. Fill this land for the Lord." And as if God had need of him, in that very moment, he vanished.

Holding a large rock, Eliab hurried toward her. "We shall mark where he stood with stones so we will remember God's goodness."

"I am in need of a tower to keep me on my feet." She stilled and turned in the direction of Isa's dwelling and touched Eliab's shoulder. "Do you hear something?"

The *meh-meh-meh* grew louder.

Could it be?

She ran toward the bleating. Eliab followed close behind.

Isa's house stood anew, as did the sheep's pen.

Eliab opened the front door. A ewe brushed by him, protesting her confinement. The sheep trotted Naomi's direction.

She knew those eyes.

Naomi could barely breathe. Her heart swelled like an overfilled waterskin threatening to burst. She knelt and petted the ewe. Her ewe. The mother's muzzle preened upward as if she wanted her throat scratched.

"My gift. He restored my wedding gift." She rubbed her hands up and down each leg. "There is not a blemish on her."

"Wait until Isa sees your sheep." Eliab grinned so wide his smirk reminded her of Hamul's mask.

"The ewe is ours. You gave her to me."

"Only after much protest." He knelt. "How could I carry you and the livestock to the top of the ravine?"

Reaching up, Naomi stroked her husband's beard. With each caress a petal-soft flutter twirled inside her body. "Will the mother be safe in the sheep's pen?"

His hand settled on her hip. "The trough is full and there is fodder."

"And our friends? Will they return soon?" She gazed into Eliab's eyes, her reflection overshadowing the brown pools so deep she could dive into them. She did not want him to think her wanton, but she was ready to become his wife in every way and fulfill her promise to be fruitful.

"Our family does not know there is anything to return to." Eliab stroked the contour of her face. "And I believe they will join the elders for a meal."

The ewe nibbled at her garment, grazing her knees. She giggled at the tickle. "I am not hungry, husband."

He tipped her chin so all she could see was him. "But I am."

29

Naomi climbed the ladder to Eliab's bedroom. Her bedroom. Their bedroom. With every rung she touched, her palms dampened, and her heartbeat pulsed at her throat where Eliab had kissed her in the cave. When she reached the threshold, she halted and scanned the room. Everything had stayed the same—the washbasin, the bed, and her loom. Gratitude flooded her soul. She practically leapt across the floor when she spied the wooden frame.

Eliab stationed the ladder against the wall. "We do not need any guests to share in this moment."

She strummed her fingers over the woven pattern and envisioned the delight on Jael's face. "Not one thread of my design is different."

God had restored her ewe and her loom, but they had first been gifts from her husband, from her Eliab. The more she thought of him, of their bond, the bloom in her belly blossomed. A powerful desire unfolded within her.

"You are right, husband. We do not need any company for a while."

Removing his robe, Eliab stepped toward the loom, wearing only his loincloth and a look so precious and passionate she could hardly remain upright.

"Stay where you are." She hid behind her unfinished weave. "Wash yourself in the basin."

Hurt flashed across his features. He dipped a cloth

in the water. "I do not want to rush you. I want you to be comfortable with me."

She stripped off her head covering and cast it to the ground, welcoming the weight of her hair upon her shoulders. "I want to be with you." Her cloak slipped from her arms and fell to the floor. She shimmied out of her robe. Only the weave of her hands restored on the loom obstructed his view of her nakedness. "I want you washed so you can wash me."

Water sloshed from the washbasin. "As you wish."

Her heart pounded in a crazed rhythm with expectation of what waited in the marriage bed.

"You're beautiful. I've felt your form beside me, but for this vision, I have no words."

"Your vision is not complete." *God, I need the courage to step away from this loom.* She didn't think too long. The boom of her heart deafened deep thought. With a quick sidestep, she revealed herself, fully, and strolled toward the man she loved.

Eliab held out his hand. He stroked her cheek and brushed her hair behind her ear, his gaze never faltering or dipping below her face. Wherever he touched, her chin, her cheekbone, her lips, the sensation lingered long after he had moved on.

Her pulse raced like a chariot as he swept a sponge below the nape of her neck and dared to plunge lower. His hand paused above her breast. She willed him to hurry, but he leaned down and kissed her, not deep and desperate, but with a gentleness and a promise of what was to come.

She broke their kiss. "Please hurry, my husband." Taking his hand, she tried to move it across her belly, but his hand did not budge.

"Oh no, wife." His denial rumbled deep in his

chest. “There is no feast or festival outside, but this is a celebration, and I have only begun to watch you dance.”

Epilogue

Three years later

Naomi sat cross-legged in the shade in front of her home, spinning the wool she had carded. Her daughter twirled a piece of yarn round and round until she plopped to the ground, her eyes wide and wild. Young boys chased one another outside the cooking courtyard, whipping empty slings in the air, waging a play battle.

"Enough," Cuzbi chastised. "With all this commotion I have scorched the bread."

Again. Naomi smiled at her friend's excuse and watched her son, Micah, halt his mock slinging and squint into the flatlands. His hand cupped his brow and he stood as still as a scout while his cousin claimed victory.

"Mother." Micah raced toward her, his sling dragging in the dirt. "People coming."

She deposited her spinner in a basket and struggled to rise. Her unborn child rounded her belly, making where her feet landed a mystery. Lifting Miriam onto her hip, she waddled past the courtyard.

Three mules approached. Two with riders and one without.

Turning to Micah, she said, "We have visitors. Run to your uncle Isa's and call your father."

Micah raced toward Isa's home, arms pumping

faster than his feet could carry him. Cuzbi's son pursued his cousin like this was a new game.

Cuzbi leaned on the stone wall surrounding the cooking fire. "Isa will not leave Jael. Her birthing time is near."

"These strangers are probably in need of shelter." Naomi repositioned Miriam, who snuggled into her side.

"I hope they are not hungry." Cuzbi swiped her hands together to remove the traces of ash.

Naomi lumbered out to greet the travelers. As they grew closer, she stilled.

She knew those stripes, those seams, the stitching on those robes.

Her breathing stuttered as if all the dust the animals had kicked up had settled in her chest. Her heart pounded against her ribs as tingling pressure built behind her eyes.

"Mother." The word caught in her throat. She had not uttered it in years. But she had not forgotten her family. How many times had she spoken the wisdom of her mother to Micah and Miriam, made the food her mother taught her, and hummed the choruses her mother had cherished?

Awkward as it was with Miriam's face buried in her shoulder, she ran.

"*Abba.* Father." Tears streamed down her cheeks, seeping into her mouth, and leaving salt to sizzle on her tongue.

Her mother scrambled from her mule. Naomi embraced her, drawing her mother close.

"You came." Naomi caressed her mother's arm, reassuring herself that these travelers were not a vision. "Many times I have looked to the north and wished you to appear from the hills. I never got to say my *shalom*. You kissed me before the dance and I never kissed you back. My prayer was that we would meet again this side of heaven."

"My child, I knew we would see each other, for you never left me." Her mother pressed a hand to Naomi's belly. "God has blessed you." And with a caress to Miriam's cheek, her mother smiled brighter than a gemstone. "I would know this child. She is our granddaughter, for she is the image of you cradled on my hip."

Miriam clutched Naomi's tunic and stared, wide-eyed, at the woman who had wailed.

"It is all well, my sweet daughter." Her mother stroked Miriam's hair. The lilt in her mother's voice was welcomed like a treasured song. "Your grandmother is here to comfort you."

"And her grandfather." Heriah led the mules closer.

"Your granddaughter's name is Miriam, for she hid behind her brother, Micah. God blessed me two-fold when I thought to birth but one child."

"You will have another." Her mother patted Naomi's burgeoning belly.

"Yes, and if it is a son, he shall bear the names of my brothers who were lost to us."

Tears welled in her mother's eyes.

"How is Nadab?" An ache weighed upon Naomi's chest. Her brother's anger and hard heart tormented her at times. But only at the times she let herself remember.

Her mother's brow furrowed. "He has found a wife and they have a son. But it is not the same as one's daughter giving birth." Biting her lip, her mother could not hold back another wave of tears.

"I am glad he has an heir. That we have an heir." She squeezed her mother's hands and helped wipe the wetness from her face.

"I could not live with a woman whose grief did not end." Her father came to console his wife. The familiar scent of soil and hyssop filled the air. "We waited for you to come to us. We received your gifts from the messenger and prayed you would one day come back to Shiloh. I see now it would not have been easy with the size of your flocks and the size of your family."

"I wanted to come, but we did not know if it would be safe." She kissed Miriam as a reminder of her blessing.

"There is wisdom in your thinking. For some, it is still difficult to welcome a Benjamite, especially if that man has received blessings." Her father glanced off into the distance. "We both know of one."

Naomi turned to see Eliab and Micah approaching. Her son seemed more interested in a narrow stick he had found than in the two visitors speaking with his mother.

Eliab hurried to her side. He nodded to her father. "Heriah, I am grateful you traveled to our home."

Her father nodded. "You have a tall son. He will be able to assist you with your herds."

Her heart budded with joy at her father's praise.

"And he is strong like his grandfather." Eliab embraced Heriah. "You are welcome in this place. We have several children afoot."

Micah reached toward the sky and extended his branch, chastising the clouds.

Her mother and father laughed.

Her father knelt next to Micah. "If you like to dig in the dirt, I have something for you." Heriah hurried toward the third mule and opened a large sack. He pulled out a handful of dirt with a green shoot embedded in the soil. "I have brought the start of a vineyard to Gibeah." Heriah let his grandson poke at the plant. Not to be outdone, Miriam fidgeted her way out of Naomi's arms and into her grandfather's. "Your mother grew up picking grapes."

"She is a woman of many talents." Eliab's hand dropped to the small of her back. "You have bestowed on me a priceless gift."

Heriah lifted his grandson. "You and Miriam will help me plant the vines so everyone will know a seed from Ephraim blossoms here."

"Our seed." Her mother's eyes glistened.

She embraced her mother again and pulled Eliab into their sweet reunion.

"God bestows the best fruit," she whispered.

Eliab caressed her belly. "We have been blessed with a bountiful harvest."

"You have," her mother added. "And now I want to hold my granddaughter."

As her mother bent to speak with Miriam, Eliab enfolded Naomi into his arms.

Gazing into her husband's eyes so rich and deep with a reassuring love, Naomi reached up and sneaked one of their celebratory kisses.

Thank you…

for purchasing this Harbourlight title. For other inspirational stories, please visit our on-line bookstore at www.pelicanbookgroup.com.

For questions or more information, contact us at customer@pelicanbookgroup.com.

Harbourlight Books
The Beacon in Christian Fiction™
an imprint of Pelican Book Group
www.pelicanbookgroup.com

Connect with Us
www.facebook.com/Pelicanbookgroup
www.twitter.com/pelicanbookgrp

To receive news and specials, subscribe to our bulletin
http://pelink.us/bulletin

May God's glory shine through
this inspirational work of fiction.

AMDG

You Can Help!

At Pelican Book Group it is our mission to entertain readers with fiction that uplifts the Gospel. It is our privilege to spend time with you awhile as you read our stories.

We believe you can help us to bring Christ into the lives of people across the globe. And you don't have to open your wallet or even leave your house!

Here are 3 simple things you can do to help us bring illuminating fiction™ to people everywhere.

1) If you enjoyed this book, write a positive review. Post it at online retailers and websites where readers gather. And share your review with us at reviews@pelicanbookgroup.com (this does give us permission to reprint your review in whole or in part.)

2) If you enjoyed this book, recommend it to a friend in person, at a book club or on social media.

3) If you have suggestions on how we can improve or expand our selection, let us know. We value your opinion. Use the contact form on our web site or e-mail us at customer@pelicanbookgroup.com

God Can Help!

Are you in need? The Almighty can do great things for you. Holy is His Name! He has mercy in every generation. He can lift up the lowly and accomplish all things. Reach out today.

Do not fear: I am with you; do not be anxious: I am your God. I will strengthen you, I will help you, I will uphold you with my victorious right hand.

~Isaiah 41:10 (NAB)

We pray daily, and we especially pray for everyone connected to Pelican Book Group—that includes you! If you have a specific need, we welcome the opportunity to pray for you. Share your needs or praise reports at http://pelink.us/pray4us

Free Book Offer

We're looking for booklovers like you to partner with us! Join our team of influencers today and periodically receive free eBooks!

For more information
Visit http://pelicanbookgroup.com/booklovers